Be Afraid!

Tales of Horror Selected by
EDO VAN BELKOM

Published in Canada by Tundra Books, *McClelland & Stewart Young Readers*,
481 University Avenue, Toronto, Ontario M5G 2E9

Published in the United States by Tundra Books of Northern New York,
P.O. Box 1030, Plattsburgh, New York 12901

Library of Congress Catalog Number: 00-131204

Canadian Cataloguing in Publication Data

Main entry under title:

Be afraid! : tales of horror

ISBN 0-88776-496-7

1. Children's stories, Canadian (English).*   2. Children's stories,
American.   3. Horror tales, Canadian (English).*   4. Horror tales,
American.   I. Van Belkom, Edo.

PS8323.H67B4 2000   JC813.08738089282   C00-930405-3
PR9197.35.H67B4 2000

We acknowledge the support of the Canada Council for the Arts and the
Ontario Arts Council for our publishing program.

We acknowledge the financial support of the Government of Canada
through the Book Publishing Industry Development Program for our
publishing activities.

Design by Terri-Anne Fong

Printed and bound in Canada

1 2 3 4 5 6   05 04 03 02 01 00

To my son, Luke

CONTENTS

Foreword: An Invitation to Be Afraid!

Edo van Belkom

What scares you?

What is it that causes you to be afraid?

Is it vampires? Werewolves? Evil demons?

Sure, those things can be scary, but no one has ever really seen a vampire walking down Main Street, and no one ever runs for cover at the sight of a full moon. If people did, this book would be full of stories about ghouls and goblins and things that go bump in the night. But it's not, because horror is not about monsters – it's about people's personal fears and emotions.

So while there are a few supernatural goings-on in this book, they serve only as a catalyst for the real horror that rises up from the darkness of our everyday lives.

In this book, you will . . .

Be Afraid! of the changes that occur to young bodies as they grow into adulthood.

Be Afraid! of the stranger in your house who also happens to be the newest member of the family.

Be Afraid! of wanting something so badly that you end up

paying the ultimate price just to have it.

Be Afraid! for a girl who is teased and ridiculed for having a scar that has ruined her otherwise pretty face.

Be Afraid! of always being picked last in gym class . . . of losing someone you love, only to learn you didn't know her at all . . . of getting caught up in an old man's memories of a long-ago war . . . of guns and the people who deal in death.

These are the kinds of real-life terrors you'll find here, the ones that can happen to you, or someone close to you.

So let's take a trip through the darker part of the world around us.

And don't worry.

If you're not afraid yet . . . you will be.

Jake's Body

Steve Rasnic Tem

Jake couldn't tell you the exact day it all changed – it had been a sometimes change, an every-once-in-a-while change. It had been a slow summer. Sometimes something new would happen, but most of the time he was bored sick. He was a teenager now, but being a teenager didn't feel as special as he'd thought it would. He did have more freedom – his mom and dad let him ride his bike almost as far as he wanted to. Once he'd ridden his bike into a part of town so different from his own it had scared him a little, so that he was glad when he got back home. Of course, he couldn't tell his parents he'd been scared.

But except for Jake's bike trips, each day just seemed to be the same day, repeated over and over again. It had been a hot summer, the hottest summer in years according to the weatherman. Jake didn't know about that. What he did know was that practically every day was like taking a hot shower with your clothes on.

He guessed there had been signs all summer that something different was about to happen. For example, his mom and dad had been acting pretty weird. They'd started complaining that his feet smelled all the time, and that he didn't take baths often enough. He couldn't smell anything different, so what was the problem? Besides, he figured *his* smell, *his* business. He never asked his mom and dad if *they* took baths every day.

Then his mom got mad because he didn't like what she cooked anymore. She was always making things with cheese and sauces and vegetables, and all he ever wanted were burgers and fries. He couldn't help it that he liked burgers and fries. He was a meat eater! He could eat them all day — the greasier the better.

And his dad had been pretty grumpy. His dad had to work long hours to buy food for them all, and he didn't like it when Jake wouldn't eat his mother's cooking. "You're a smart kid," his dad had said. "You should eat better."

"Smart as a fox," Jake had replied. He didn't know what that meant, but more and more lately he'd been saying stuff like that, silly stuff, so that his mom and dad looked at him as if he were crazy. "Crazy like a fox," he'd say to himself in the mirror.

But he knew he wasn't — lots of his friends said silly stuff like that. Sometimes one of his teachers would say, "Act your age." But Jake figured he already was.

His dad wanted to spend more time with Jake that summer, but Jake almost never felt like it. So now Jake and his dad didn't talk much. Jake guessed they were kind of mad at each other.

Then Jake got this job down at the animal hospital for the last part of the summer. He mostly had to feed the dogs and cats they boarded, but sometimes he helped with an operation or two. He'd come home soaking wet, with that hot animal smell on him, and he'd make himself take a long, cool bath, but he still smelled bad. And that gave his parents a reason to complain even more.

Jake stopped seeing his friends because he didn't want them to know he smelled. He stayed home watching TV, eating chocolate bars, and ordering in pizza, even though zits were popping out everywhere.

So he was smelly and he ate too much junk and he had a billion zits all over him and his parents were mad at him and now his friends were mad at him and he didn't like taking care of those gross-looking cats and dogs anymore, but Jake figured at least the rest of the summer couldn't be so bad. Everything that could go wrong had already gone wrong, right?

Then he woke up one Saturday morning with hair growing on his knees.

Now, he'd noticed that he'd been getting more hair in his pits and other places, but he was dark-haired, and this new hair was a pretty red. He sat on his bed for almost an hour, and the hair on his knees grew and grew until it was several inches long. Bright red hair like a fox's. Jake was so surprised he started laughing, but when he stood in front of the mirror, with these red beards hanging down a couple of inches from his knees, well, that wasn't so funny. He wasn't shaving yet, although his dad said it was probably only a couple of months away, so he went into his parents' bathroom and took a razor. He started to shave his left knee, but a mouth full of sharp teeth suddenly appeared in his kneecap and bit the razor in half.

Jake didn't know what to do. He had to be at work in a half-hour. He probably should've gone to the hospital right then and there, but he was too embarrassed. He heard his mom and dad talking downstairs and thought about going down and telling them, but he just couldn't. They'd tell him that that was what happened when you ate junk and didn't take baths very much, and he just knew that if they said that stuff to him, he'd probably start howling and bite one of them, and as much as they made him mad sometimes, he really didn't want to hurt either one of them.

So Jake wrapped a bandage over the knee that had the mouth and slipped into his jeans. He could feel that mouth squirming under the bandage, and he heard it making a soft growling sound, but he didn't think anyone else could hear it.

The worst thing was that every time the mouth in his knee growled, Jake wanted to growl, too. And that made him think foxy thoughts about chasing chickens and eating raw meat, and that just about made him sick.

He hoped the mouth wouldn't chew through the bandage and then through his brand-new jeans. He hoped a mouth didn't show up in his other knee. He hoped his parents didn't find out he had red beards and mouths growing on his knees. He didn't know what they would do — his mom would probably call the doctor or something and his dad would probably ask all kinds of personal questions about what Jake was doing with his spare time. He hoped a lot of things, but he had to go to work.

So that's exactly what he did. He tried not to think about what was happening to his body.

Luckily, it was a slow day at the vet hospital: just a few cats and dogs to spay so they couldn't have kids, a cocker with worms, and an old beagle they had to put to sleep. But it was a hot day, the air conditioner was broken, and by noon Jake could hardly stand it. His legs were on fire. During his lunch break, he sneaked into the bathroom and took off his pants.

A small fox foot with long claws was growing out of his left leg.

At first, Jake didn't recognize it as a foot: the toes were short and stubby, and the claws were so pale they were almost invisible. But then the claws started moving, scratching up and down his leg as if the fox foot wanted to run somewhere.

Jake put his pants back on and went back to work. What else was he supposed to do? The vet wasn't going to let him off work early just because he had a fox foot growing out of his leg.

It wasn't too comfortable a day for Jake. The fox mouth on his knee kept trying to chew through the bandage; the red beards kept growing longer and making his legs itch; and the fox foot kept clawing the inside of his jeans, making tiny rips that someone was bound to notice sooner or later. He spent the entire afternoon scratching and jumping and yanking up his jeans.

At the end of the day, Jake rode his bike home (which wasn't easy – the claws kept sneaking out of the bottom of his pant leg and untying his shoestring). When he walked into the house, he just waved his parents off. He tried to tell them that he wasn't hungry, that he was too tired and all he wanted to do was go to bed and sleep. But the minute he opened his mouth these weird animal sounds started coming out, so he shut his mouth and ran up the stairs. He felt like getting down on his hands and knees, but he stopped himself.

His dad grumbled something under his breath and his mom called out, "Hope you feel better, honey." But neither one of them followed him up the stairs to his room, which was a good thing. He still understood what they were saying, but it was getting harder and harder.

Just as soon as he got into his room and shut his door, Jake tore his clothes off and stood in front of the mirror on his closet door. The mouth had chewed through the bandage, but the fox foot had stuck itself into the mouth, so the mouth seemed happy enough. And the red beards had pretty much stopped growing. They'd wrapped themselves around part of each leg, so that now they looked like bright red wool scarves, only worn in a funny place.

But two huge eyes, like an animal's eyes, with these big, soft lids had appeared in the middle of his chest. And they kept looking at him in the mirror as if they wanted him to do something.

Jake didn't want to do anything. He just wanted things to get boring again. He just wanted to go to sleep. So he crawled into bed and pulled the covers over his head and closed his eyes and tried to think of something peaceful. But the eyes in his chest kept blinking and blinking, and they were so big that every time they blinked they made his whole body jerk.

Finally, Jake gave up and climbed out of bed. He was so tired he didn't know what to do. He started walking back and forth across the room, staring at himself in the mirror each time he passed his closet door.

But walking back and forth like that just made him more and more nervous. And the more nervous he got, the madder he got that his parents couldn't help him. And the madder he got, the more he itched. He looked at himself in the mirror again, and now he had a beard on his face! He could see the red beard growing down his chin and down his chest at an amazing rate, covering the rest of his body completely, so that soon it looked as if he were wearing a red fur coat. If his mom and dad saw him like this, they'd have a fit!

Jake walked closer to the mirror and took a good look at his face. Two huge fox eyes stared back out of a face that looked a lot – but not totally – like his own. Under these eyes was a big nose with dark hairs, and under that was a mouth filled with enormous, sharp teeth.

"I look stupid!" he shouted at his mirror. Although the words didn't sound much like English anymore.

Shouting was a pretty silly thing to do. His dad called from downstairs, "What's going *on* up there?"

"Nothing! Jake tried to say. "Sorry! Don't come up!" But all his mouth would do was yip, snap, and snarl, and he kept biting his tongue, which felt too big for his mouth.

Don't come up! Real smart, Jake. He couldn't believe he'd actually tried to say that.

Then to his horror, Jake's goofy-looking body started doing a goofy-looking dance, the long, bare legs with huge, ugly feet kicking up left and right, as high as his head, and the long arms with the twisted, ugly elbows waving loosely back and forth like flags at a football game. "Hey, hey, hey!" the ugly mouth on his goofy head shouted, its long pink tongue rolling out and licking Jake's reflection. "Hey, hey, hey!" Jake felt like he was in a cartoon.

"Jake! What's that noise?" his dad called up again.

Jake couldn't shut himself up. Every time he tried to cover his mouth with his hands, his own mouth bit them as hard as it could. He was so embarrassed that he wanted to scream. He was so embarrassed that the red fox hair on his body started growing again, covering his face and his arms and the rest of him until all you could see were his big, bright eyes and his big, terrible mouth.

"*Jake!*" That was both his mom and his dad shouting together now. What was he going to tell them? How was he going to explain this?

Jake was so embarrassed that he started to bark. Jake was so embarrassed that he started to growl and snap like a fox. Long hair kept getting into his mouth and he had to spit it out.

"Jake!" His parents were beating on his door now. There was no use trying to hide it. He got down on his hands and knees, trotted over to the door, and started opening it. He'd tell them everything, even if they thought he was crazy. They were his mom and dad – they might know what to do. He closed his eyes and threw the door open all the way.

"Jake, are you sick? What's wrong with you, son?"

Jake opened his eyes and looked at his father's concerned face. He looked at his mother's worried frown. He opened his mouth to say something, but nothing came out. Why weren't they screaming? He looked like a monster!

When they still hadn't reacted after a few seconds, Jake looked down at his body. It was a little older, a little hairier maybe, but still pretty normal, he guessed.

He cleared his throat. He tried to make a smile with his lips. He didn't know if it had worked or not. "Guess I'll have some dinner after all. Guess I'm pretty hungry," he said. "Um . . . I'll just get a few more clothes on and I'll be right down." His parents didn't say anything, so he shut his door.

He dressed his body in normal school clothes and went downstairs for dinner with his family.

"Nice to have you join us," his dad said nervously.

"Have a . . . bad dream, sweetheart?" his mother asked softly.

Jake mumbled something about a cold, sat down, and began eating his roast beef, baked potato, and peas. When he finished that, he asked for second helpings on everything. Then when he finished that, he started to ask for more, but he stopped himself when he saw the nervous look in his mother's eyes. "Good meal, Mom," he said quickly, and she smiled a little. He looked around the table. He felt like grabbing his mom's plate and eating everything off that, then going after his dad's plate and eating everything off that. He could barely stop himself.

"Something wrong, Jake?" his dad asked. "You look a little uncomfortable."

"It's nothing, Dad. Just a little itch," Jake said, feeling the big fox tail trying to push its way out of the back of his pants.

The Witch of the Dawn

Ed Greenwood

A door whined upward like something out of a flying-saucer movie, and a dude busy fooling himself that he was cool got out of his red sports car, oh-so-elegant leather jacket rippling. He was wearing mirrored sunglasses, of course, despite the almost-black sky, the driving rain it was enthusiastically dispensing, and the thick mist curling past me like cigar smoke in a hurry to get elsewhere.

He looked up at the sign that was giving me light enough to work by with something like disbelief in his sneer – for all the world as if he'd never seen a sign with four or five holes in it before, and in hunting country, too – and spat on Dad's dock before he strode forward. Hell, *my* dock, at least for a week or so, until Dad was up and around again.

I gave him an expressionless nod – two can play at being cool, City Dude – and went back to fishing fouled plugs out of places that took skin off knuckles. His expensive boots clacked slowly across the dock with the swagger that comes from watching too many idiots with attitude in too many movies, and he stopped beside me.

About then, the last plug reluctantly surrendered its grip and fell into my hand – in pieces – so I looked up. His eyes, too close to mine, were still hidden behind shades that reflected back to me the grease-covered Evinrude I was working on.

"You Elmer?"

I shook my head. "He's my dad," I told him, wiping my hands on a rag. "I'm Fred. Fred Risrick." I waved the rag at the rain-slicked docks and the carcasses of long-dead motors around us, and played at being Dad for a moment, drawl and all. "Anything I can help you with?" I left off the "mister" Dad would've used. Some dudes just don't deserve it.

Mr. City Dude didn't bother to survey my domain. His chin tilted as those hidden eyes traveled slowly back up to the sign, and the sneer slowly grew – or rather, I was beginning to figure, returned to its habitual force. He even stepped back to give Dad's sign a good, long look, as if to underscore his . . . well, "derisive incredulity," one of the books I'd been reading would've called it. "Being a prick," my friends from school would've said.

I shrugged. Elmer's Old Axe Marina had been good enough for Dad, and it was good enough for me. Folks didn't come into the shop to look at the scenery, anyhow. The only calendar Dad had up, by Norman Rockwell, sported ladies painted with their clothes on – and since old Myra'd left, they were the only ladies of any sort around the place.

No, folks came here in a hurry to get into their boats and out into the scenery yonder, though in all the rain right now you could barely see the far side of the lake and the channel where Big Buck Lake branched off. The mist hid the whole length of Hook Lake in the other direction like a wall of shadow, though I could see a few lights from Wolf Narrows.

A lot of country out there, and more of it twinkling with cottages every year.

Still enough country to get lost in, though. Darcy and Barr, Old Doc Henty, and Ralph Carlisle – others, too. One after another, down the years. Vanished, every one of them. All after they'd bought Milt Hemberson's place . . . which, unless I missed my guess, was what City Dude here had just done.

Make that Cheap City Dude. Merla Barr had let it go for thirty grand – forty acres and all – and Jean Darcy had listed it at twenty-seven. A quarter of what most shacks around here went for now – but then, no one around here wanted to add himself to the list of those who'd disappeared.

Milt Hemberson had been an inventor, and long before he'd died there'd been plenty of stories about his nasty sense of humor and the booby traps all over his land. There'd been dogs killed and even a kid, some said, though I couldn't believe that could've happened without police and all.

Hmmph. Milt had been one of the those great guys who treated young kids – like I'd been then – as people and not little slaves or furniture to be ignored. Dad had told me to call him Uncle Milt, but he'd growled, "None of that crap, Elm. I'm Milt and he's Fred – we're equals." Then he'd reached out his hand to shake mine, seriously, too, as if we'd really been equals, one man to another.

Dad had turned away without saying anything, but I could tell he was pleased. Oh, yes, I could see Milt clear as day in my mind, standing right over there, leaning on the old gas pump, mouth hanging open like a panting dog in that silent laugh of his, just listening to the latest—

"I understand you have a boat here, Mr. Risrick," City Dude said uncertainly, rubbing at a line of dirt on his upper lip that he probably believed was a smart mustache, "that belongs to me."

I lifted my eyebrows, to look old and wise and give him a good look at what bristle hair *should* look like, and asked, "Yeah? Tom Darcy's boat?"

He coughed. "Ah, yes. His wife said you'd have the key."

I nodded, then pointed with my head to where the *Witch* was tied up in her Sunday collar – a cradle of tires upon tires that kept her from harm, year after year, as the winter ice shoved and jabbed at everything. Younger, less fragile boats spent the winters well away from the water, under the leaning galvanized sheds that would someday collapse on top of them and take Dad's business – and my future – with them.

"In the boat," I told him. "She's ready to go. Mrs. Darcy tell you where the cottage is?"

"Down Hook Lake, past Luck Creek," he said slowly, "then just past where Gossamer Lake begins. An old boathouse falling into the water. Blue."

I nodded. "Can't miss it." I turned away to find new plugs, waiting. I knew what he'd say next.

"Uh," he said reluctantly, staring into the rain, "which one is Hook Lake?"

I turned around slowly, giving his sneer right back to him. "This one," I told him. "Strut just two more steps and you'll be up past your ears in it."

He stiffened and went red, then white. Evidently, in his world-view, teenagers were supposed to tug their forelocks and take his contempt, not hand it back to him.

"*Listen*," he hissed, as sinister as any movie hitman, and then fell silent, coming a little slowly to the realization that he needed what I knew for at least a few days before he could be properly rude to me. He opened his mouth to say something, and then closed it again, not knowing how to go on.

Well, he'd be a customer for a little while, at least, and I'd seen Dad be as gentle as a mothering sergeant with more smart city dorks than I could remember, so I gave him a smile and pointed into the gloom. "You'll be fine, Mr. . . ."

"Kanter," he said quickly. "Scott Kanter. I'm a lawyer." He barked that last as if it were a gun he was pulling on me. I suppose he thought it was.

I just nodded, and pointed again, until his eyes followed my hand. I'd aimed to become a lawyer before Dad fell ill, back when I thought every lawyer worked in an office equipped with dozens of beautiful women who couldn't help leaping into the lawyer's bed every night before a commercial break. I bet City Dude Kanter had watched the same shows and figured every lawyer got the girls and more money than he could count in his first week on the job, then spent the rest of his career — when he wasn't out trying a new golf course — deciding which exotic resort to get laid in *this* weekend. Maybe he still thought that. Maybe he'd even live long enough to learn some things and unlearn others. I planned to.

"There are no rocks this side until you get down to Axe Island," I told him, "and that's a long way past where you're heading. So you can stay about forty feet out from shore all the way. Stay slow and use the searchlight, and you'll be all right. The *Witch* always starts when you turn the key — all I've ever had to do to her is keep the gas and oil up. Milt's place was fine when I checked on it last week. There're no bears to worry about this side of the lake since every second guy got himself a big enough gun to repel uninvited tanks, and Darcy might even have left you some food."

"Who's Milt?" he asked, frowning. "And what happened to . . . Mr. Darcy?"

I shook my head, knowing he really wanted my answer to his second question. "Just disappeared," I said. "No one's seen him."

"Is he . . . dead?"

I stared right at the expressionless shields of his shades and just shrugged.

"Why would his wife want to sell so quickly, if . . ."

I juggled the new plugs in my palm and told him the truth. "Mrs. Darcy never liked wild things and getting cold and being miles from stores that were open all night. She'd just as soon never have seen Hook Lake, and I s'pose she wants her money back – more'n half of what Tom spent to buy Milt's place was hers."

"Who's this Milt guy?" he asked again, frowning.

I went over to the wall beside the calendar and pulled a business card that didn't have too much grease on it out of the frame where Dad had stuck it years ago. The first business card I'd ever seen around these parts, come to think of it – long, long before every kid and his grandad had an Internet site and a need to tell the world his cute address.

"'Milt Hemberson, Inventor,'" he read aloud, coming over to stand under the sign. "He built the cottage?"

I nodded. "And the boat." I nodded again at the *Witch* in her Sunday collar and shone the flashlight from the hook by the door her way, making him notice the beautiful old mahogany cruiser – damned near a battleship, even if she was too old and fragile to take out of the water now.

Winter after winter cracked other boats or shattered their motors, and she just sat there in the water, Milt's mystery boat, sometimes under a foot of ice but untouched by it come spring. Ran like a watch, so long as I "left her alone," as Milt had told me to do. So that's what Dad did and I did, too, though owner after owner had complained that she was running more slowly – smoothly, but just slowing down, as if she was dragging a big weight behind her. Sooner or later, one of these jerks would run her onto rocks or have a few drinks too many and whang a few docks too hard, and the *Witch*'d be gone.

"There she is," I told Mr. Kanter the lawyer. "The *Witch of the Dawn*."

He frowned at me like I'd said a bad word. "The what? That's a . . . an odd name for a boat."

I shrugged. "Milt had a lady," I told him. "A wild one. Tanith Tezra, her name was. *She* was the Witch of the Dawn – from some folk song she liked, or something."

He shrugged and turned away, leaving me remembering Tanith. I'd never seen a woman so beautiful, not even in the magazines Dad thought he'd always managed to keep hidden from me. Eyes like black pools, legs that went on forever, a face better'n any movie star or model I could think of.

"My tigress," he'd called her. She'd be lying full length on the bow of the boat as Milt brought her into the collar, making heads snap around all over the place and setting Dad to growling. Black leather jacket always, but not much else. Black garters, fishnets and little buckle-boots, black makeup – this was back, remember, when not every six-year-old put on black everything and went out on the streets *trying* to look like a vampire or something – and silver bullets dangling from her ears on big rings. Rings that were almost as big as the ones she wore on her fingers, and that bristled with little points that made them look like black stars and drew blood whenever she smashed the face of someone a little too drunk to mind his limits. A tattoo like a crawling dragon on her belly, snaking its way clear down to where she must've got a whole lot friendlier with the guy who tattooed her than I'd've been comfortable getting.

Tanith Tezra. Oh, yes, I knew now why Dad had growled. Now, when it was too late.

More nights than not, Milt and his tigress would go out in the *Witch* after moonrise and drift on the lake when it was like smooth silver. They'd claw at each other all night long, sometimes like cats in heat and sometimes brawling. God but that Tezra lady could scream!

They'd both drink straight from the bottle – one each, and a new one every night – and fight like snarling wolves, so it was no surprise to some when Milt finally killed her. Strangled her and threw her over the side, folks said, though it was more likely she'd just fallen over the side during one of their binges and drowned. Someone down on the end of his dock one night to look at the stars had glanced down into her white, staring face drifting in the water, and had run so hard and so far while losing his supper that her body was long gone before he could gasp out what he'd seen to the guys playing cards at Ernie's, four miles away.

When they finally found her, near noon the next day, the fish had been at her face – though I don't know of any fish big enough to bite off both her arms just below the shoulders. No propeller slices on her, nothing left to tell what had killed Tanith Tezra – and they never got an answer about her out of Milt either.

He drove that boat around the lake like his very own storm, saying no word to anyone, for a day and a half. When the officers finally showed up to borrow Dad's runabout to go and talk to him, they found the *Witch* drifting down by Wolf Narrows with no one at the wheel.

No one ever saw Milt again. It'd been almost ten years before a niece showed up, just long enough to sell the place to someone from too far away to know about Milt and Tezra or to wonder whether the place was hers to sell. That some-one was Rick Hardy, and he went missing the next winter, leaving the *Witch* adrift right beside his dock.

That started the stories of lake monsters, such as the giant eel, all black and slimy, that would rear up over the side of an old and slow boat like the *Witch* and snatch someone who was alone and . . . feed. Or the worms that swarmed up fishing lines to tunnel in through the eyes and noses of dozing fishermen, eating them down to bloody sacks of bone and flesh that slumped over the side and drifted down into the weeds forever. Or the swimming bear that snatched men over the side, rods and all.

All of which did nothing to explain why the fishermen who went out in battered little aluminum Springboks every year came puttering safely back to their docks again.

Only one guy ever talked about the *Witch* being a haunted boat, and that was right after Wes Grayson went missing and Doc Henty bought Milt's place. But I'd been on her time and time again, seeing to her and bringing her back to the collar to wait for her next owner, and I'd never felt anything strange or even uneasy or noticed anything amiss beyond that one little locker under the side seats that kept popping open – an empty locker, nothing sinister. The *Witch* was a beautiful old thing, trim as black as Tanith's leather, and so responsive to the wheel (Milt had liked to troll for fish, and he wanted something that would glide along as slow as a drifting log and still heed his steering) that Doe O'Brien, all eighty-two pounds and four feet and a bit of her, had often taken her out down Big Buck for "a proper cruise," playing chase with city dudes in their speedboats among all the rocks up by the mouth of Axe Creek. She could roar along, all right, but at what Dad liked to call sane speeds she was quiet, sliding through the water almost silently, making no more sound than a little tapping, like someone's fingers drumming impatiently on something.

No, if there was something sinister behind all these dudes disappearing after buying Milt's place, it was probably up at his house. A house was what he always called it, never a cottage, and I guess not – all forty-odd rooms of it. A mansion, with cellars blasted into the rock behind it, a tower with a cupola where he'd sat reading by the light of a storm lantern, and up on the wall a moose skull (a moose head until the rats got at it one winter, but it'd been a skull for so long that I never remembered it any other way) that was bigger than some of the windows in my place. Milt had put in one of those overhead tube systems that delivered mail from room to room; he liked to give unwary guests thoroughly shaken-up beer cans and dry-laugh himself near sick when they got drenched.

His place had been full of waterbuckets that toppled on the heads of folk who opened the wrong door, doors that led nowhere, and that sort of thing. Milt had been weird, all right, and who's to say he wasn't hiding up there still, somewhere on his forty acres of breakneck bush, living off the wallets – hey, with the Net, even the credit cards – of those foolish enough to buy a cottage far too underpriced to be for real?

That I never saw a hint of his still being around the place meant nothing; he and I had always been friends, but he'd never really trusted anyone. If he was lurking, he'd have no reason to play pranks on me, and he wouldn't want to alert me to his continued presence anyway. Now, there was a mysterious float plane that came in, always after dark, down Kellerson's way, and that always left again before morn; instead of the drugs and poached bear organs most people thought it was carrying, it could be his hired supply plane. . . .

Well, perhaps Mr. Kanter the lawyer would have himself a scare or two tonight, and would tell me all about it in the morning. He'd taken one of those fancy cases out of his car, without bothering to move the vehicle from blocking my boat launch and where the milk truck usually parked, and gone off to the *Witch* without another word to me.

She'd started up at his first turn of the key – just as she always did – and he'd played with the knobs and buttons long enough to get all her lights on and see where and how to cast her off. He'd managed to turn by the shop sheds without hitting any of the listing boats moored there, and he was now being a city dude to the hilt, revving the *Witch* like an impatient kid with a muscle car at a red light, as if he were anxious to race out there into the mist and rain and get himself killed in a hurry.

He'd be back in the morning to ask how to get the pump going. Milt's system was so complicated that no one ever figured out all the steps without help, and unless Mr. Kanter happened to know where to phone Betty Grayson or Jean Darcy in Florida, he'd have no water until he talked to me. Oh, yes, he'd be in by morning.

Besides, he'd want coffee and a paper to read. Even with cellphones in both pockets, city dudes can't bear to be out of touch for more than a night, for fear they'll miss reading about something important that happened to them when they weren't looking.

The *Witch* purred out into the night, into open water. Well, at least in this storm he'd have a clear run, with no drunks running down the lake without lights, and no girls out with their guys drifting and necking.

I spat onto the dock, just where Kanter had, and went back to my work. I wanted to surprise Dad, and I was way behind, even without clever city dude lawyers showing up to waste tomorrow morning.

Lights slid across the shop wall. He'd turned about and was coming back. I plucked up the flashlight and went out to see why. If it was the giant eel, I wanted a look at it.

He shone the *Witch*'s searchlight in my face, of course, and I was still squinting when he snapped, "Nice boat. *Very* nice. But she's dragging; propeller shaft going, maybe? I'll bring her back in the morning so you can drag her right out and have a look. Don't worry, I've got plenty of money."

"But—"

He didn't wait to let me tell him about keeping old boats wet to prevent them leaking, or about Milt's commandment to "keep her in the water all the time – and I mean *all* the time; I built her like a fish, to stay wet."

"Whatever you were fixing tomorrow," he barked, every inch the master snapping orders now, "it can wait. I'll pay you double whatever you usually charge. I need a boat I can rely on if I'm going to be alone in a handyman's special of a cottage – and why else would it've been so cheap? You sell coffee, I hope."

"Some call it that," I told him, sliding into the role of lackey because it was easiest. "You an early riser, or do you let the sun get up first to light the way?"

"The latter, Mr. Risrick," he said coldly, and spun the *Witch* back out into the storm. I watched him go, as smooth and steady out into the darkness – it was full night now – as if he'd

grown up on Hook Lake. Well, hoody hoo. A new mystery for
Charlie and the other loose-jaws to worry at when they came
for their java. *"The latter, Mr. Risrick."* Hoody hoo.

The next day dawned bright and clear, with a cool breeze
sliding down the lake. Postcard weather, bad for fishing
everywhere except Hook Lake, where pickerel, trout, and
even the odd muskie didn't seem to know the rules. I could
hear the motors starting up over by Birch Point already. I'd
have to move fast to have the coffee going and get bacon on
if I wanted to sell any bacon sandwiches to the early guys like
Len Whitaker, whose wife finally left him after he tossed one
too many cold, dripping, still-gasping muskies on top of her
as she lay dozing in curlers and a Sweet Remembrances
nightie, and he bellowed cheerfully, "Look what I got us for
breakfast! Get up and get frying, woman!"

The old guys still chuckled over that one. Every morning.
Somehow even I was chuckling at it, too, one more time, as I
stamped my boots on more or less properly and headed out to
the pole to turn off the dock lights. Ever notice how electricity
grows no cheaper, no matter how many nuclear pl—

I stopped, staring. The *Witch* was drifting in the middle of
the harbor, her lights on. God's teeth, had City Dude Kanter
shut off the motor to save himself a few pennies with near a
million dollars worth of boats all around him? Well, enough
of being his little lackey! I was going to give him such a warm
and heaping load of verbal shi—

A stray wash from across the lake turned the old cruiser a
little more away from me, and I could see right along her.
Unless Mr. Kanter was lying flat on his face down in the
cabin, she was empty, with no one aboard.

I started my handyboat in a sort of daze, knowing I had to get the *Witch* tied up in a hurry, before she started banging into things, and then get to the griddle and the coffee before I lost a whole morning's business. Holy howling *hell*, wasn't there enough going wrong around here with Dad sick? I didn't need this sort of . . .

I came alongside, put my boathook around the *Witch*'s gunwale rail, and towed. She *was* empty, and yes, Kanter's car was right where he'd left it, still in the way of all my morning customers who didn't come by boat.

She was sluggish, too, riding heavy in the water, just as he'd complained about. The hell with it – the winter cradle-dolly was right here, waiting under water. I'd have her out, and if there were no holes and nothing was caught on her, I'd let go the winch and she'd be back in the water, but safely docked in the dolly, until the lunch lull, when I could grab a few minutes to look her over properly.

The chains rattled into place, the winch started without hesitation, and the *Witch* started up onto dry land for the first time since her launching, so far as I knew. Had old Hemberson built some sort of special hull? I'd always wondered.

There were channels dug away in her sides, aft, and huge bolts in them, all green with weed. Bolts that dragged cables behind them, trolling cables! Well, that explained the drag. Something was caught on—

The something was a body, more bone than anything else now, but still wearing the red sweater that had been Carl O'Brien's. The cable ran on past the hook caught in his ribs, though, and there was something shapeless – someone – on the other side, too, lower down. On the next hook.

God, there were hooks every ten feet, and what was left of a guy on each one.

I barely noticed Kanter, hooked and staring at the end of the starboard cable. By then, I'd seen what was caught on the otherwise empty first hook on the port side. An old commodore's cap, its gold piping washed out to sickly yellow. Milt Hemberson's cap.

Fighting down the urge to be really sick, I slapped the winch into reverse, hoping to get the whole mess under water before any of the java-lovers came into the harbor. Sweet shuddering Christ, everyone knew I looked after the *Witch — everyone!*

I'd be answering cold questions from oh-so-polite cops before lunchtime for sure, and Dad would be ruined without ever getting up from his sickbed. My only hope was to get the *Witch* back into her collar and somehow keep those trolling lines deep down under, where no one could get tangled in them or see what was hooked onto them. And somehow figure out who was using the *Witch* to murder men before that person knew what I'd found and came after *me*.

I was cursing like I'd never cursed before. The *Witch* started at my first turn of her key and purred under me like an old friend. I started to think I just might make it back to the collar, where I could shove this nightmare under a stone to worry about later.

Stones! That's what I needed! Milt's anchor stones! Two boulders, painted gold in one of his weird moods and attached to long cables for use as storm anchors. They'd been stowed in lockers along the side here . . .

I scrabbled among the seats, seeking door latches and cursing anew.

One door swung crazily, already open, and something scuttled away from under my boot like a crafty crab. It'd been racing to rejoin its mate in the locker — something that was quivering and making a sound like fingers drumming.

Something that was emerging now, crawling slowly toward me as the one I'd almost stepped on turned around to advance with it, side by side like two crabs – and I got my first good look at them.

They moved purposefully forward into the light: a pair of skeletal human hands, fingerwalking, the rings on their bony fingers bristling like black stars.

The Boy Who
Loved "The Twilight Zone"

Richard Laymon

B y the heavy sound of the footfalls, Chuck knew without looking that his father had just come down the stairway and entered the basement den. Entered and halted just inside the doorway.

Chuck, on the sofa, didn't turn around. Though he kept his eyes on the television, he could no longer follow the story. Not with his father standing back there.

Finally, his father spoke. "I hope you're not planning to sit in front of the boob tube watching that nonsense all night."

"It isn't nonsense, Dad. It's a 'Twilight Zone' marathon."

"A bunch of reruns," his father said.

"They're classics."

"They're reruns. This is the one where the old babe has the Martians in her attic, only they turn out to be American astronauts, right?"

"Yeah. It's one of the really great—"

"You've seen it, Chuck. *I've* seen it. *Everyone's* seen it. You're fifteen years old, and you're sitting alone in the den on Halloween night watching a goddamn rerun on the boob tube. Your mother and I want you to get out of that chair and do something."

Chuck's throat tightened. Tears came into his eyes. On the television screen, Agnes Moorehead got blurry. "Okay," he said.

"Turn that thing off and come upstairs and join the human race."

"Okay."

He clicked the remote and the screen went dead.

"That's better. Now come on up."

Chuck listened to the footsteps of his father leaving the den and climbing the stairs. Then he sat there, sniffed, and wiped his eyes. He sure didn't want anyone to know he'd cried over missing a television show.

Not just any television show, he thought. "The Twilight Zone." The marathon. "Twilight Zones" from dusk till dawn. And now I'll have to miss them.

They don't get it. They just don't get it.

From upstairs came the sound of the doorbell. Then footsteps. Then a collection of kid voices chanting, "Trick or treat!"

Then he heard his mother saying, "And what have we here? A Dracula and a ghost and . . ."

Chuck stood up and went into the bathroom. He checked his face. His eyes still looked a little shiny and pink, but it wasn't that obvious he'd been crying.

He flicked off the light and went upstairs.

His mother was bending over to set the tray of Halloween candy on the table beside the front door. His father, in a far corner of the living room, was studying a copy of *Sports Illustrated*.

"So what do you want me to do?" Chuck asked.

His father looked up from the magazine.

His mother said, "How about helping me pass out candy?"

"Oh, what fun."

From his father's corner of the room, he heard, "You can lose the attitude, young man."

"It's Halloween, Charles. You should have fun."

"I was having fun."

"Watching reruns on the monkey box," his father said.

"It was 'The Twilight Zone.'"

Looking a little sad, his mother said, "Wouldn't you like to do something . . . real?"

"It *is* real. Watching it is. I want to be a writer!"

"We know that, dear."

You may know it, he thought, but you don't get it.

He said, "I've gotta watch stuff like that . . . and read all those books you think are so weird and everything . . . I've gotta! But every time I sit down to do something like that, you and Dad try to stop me. I've gotta mow the lawn or clean up my room or . . . or hand out candy to a bunch of stupid kids in lame-ass costumes."

"Watch your language, young man," Dad said.

"We just think you need to spend more time doing things, honey."

He sighed. Then he said, "Yeah. Okay. I know. I'm supposed to run around and act like a normal kid my age. I get it. So is it okay if I go out like a normal kid my age and do some trick-or-treating?"

His parents both stared at him.

After a while, his mother said, "I think that sounds like a fine idea. What sort of costume . . . ?"

"I've got it on," he said. He was wearing a heavy plaid shirt, blue jeans, and Reeboks.

His father frowned. "What sort of costume is that?"

"I'll go around as me."

"Brilliant."

"Why don't you put together a real costume?" his mother asked. "You say you want to be a writer – why don't you come up with something imaginative?"

"That is imaginative," his father said. "An imaginary costume. But if he isn't embarrassed . . . Heck, let him go out looking like that."

"Thanks," Chuck muttered.

"Trick or treat, my butt," Chuck said to himself as he walked along the sidewalk. His mother had given him a brown paper bag for holding the candy, but he had no intention of using it.

I'll just wander around and observe, he thought. That's what writers do – they observe.

As he roamed the sidewalks and crossed the roads, he watched how the dry brown leaves tumbled through the air. He listened to the way they crackled under his shoes when he stepped on them. He smelled the sharp, sweet tang of smoke from fireplace chimneys. He saw jack-o'-lanterns on the porches of the houses he passed, their smiling faces bright with orange candlelight.

And kids. Kids everywhere – in pairs, in small groups and large groups – scurrying from house to house. He heard them laugh and shout, heard doorbells ring, listened as the kids called out, "Trick or treat!"

Having a great time.

He used to have a great time himself, dressing up for Halloween and going from house to house with his elder brother and their friends. Shouting "Trick or treat!" Never knowing who would come to the door. Never knowing what he might be given, but feeling a tug of delight at the soft thud it made when it landed in the bottom of his bag.

Somehow, though, the excitement had dwindled with almost every year. Dressing up for Halloween had become a boring routine, going from house to house a chore.

A couple of years ago, a snotty old fart at one of the houses had said to Chuck's brother, "Aren't you a little too old to be doing this?"

"He's right," Bill had said afterward. "I'm too old for this crap."

"Me too," Chuck had said.

And that had been that.

Now, he thought, I'm supposed to go trick-or-treating all by myself just so I can look like I'm doing something instead of wasting my life in front of the television.

He'd already been forced to miss the last half of "The Invaders."

"Sucks," he muttered.

He wondered how much longer he would have to stay out.

Long enough to make it look good, he supposed. At least an hour.

Two more episodes.

What makes you think they'll let you watch it when you do get back?

Especially if you go home without any candy.

He could already hear the suspicion in his mother's voice: What were you *really* doing out there?

I have to get my hands on some candy.

Briefly, he considered hiking over to the Speed-D-Mart and buying some Halloween candy . . . just pick up a bunch of different kinds and toss them into his bag. Deceitful, but it might work.

If only he'd remembered his wallet.

Very briefly, it crossed his mind that he could steal candy from a trick-or-treater or two. He'd heard of big kids taking

Halloween candy from little kids . . . and he despised anyone who would do something that rotten.

I'll have to start ringing doorbells.

Fifteen years old, big for his age, and no costume . . . Chuck didn't even consider approaching a house by himself. The mere thought of it made him feel sick inside.

Aren't you a little old for this nonsense?

What sort of costume is *that*?

Maybe even, Whatsa matter with you? Get outta here! Go on, get outta here before I call the cops!

But if I'm with a group of kids . . .

For the next few minutes, Chuck searched for a likely bunch. All the very small children were being taken around by their parents. The somewhat older kids seemed to be guarded by teenage brothers or sisters . . . but not always.

Soon, he found seven or eight kids traveling together. Some were taller than others, but they were all significantly shorter than Chuck. He doubted that any were older than ten or eleven.

Feeling a strange mixture of excitement and fear, he began to follow them. He closed in slowly, holding back while they went to a couple of houses. As they started up the driveway toward another, he picked up his pace. None of the kids seemed to notice his approach.

He followed them onto the front porch.

Though the porch light was dark, a jack-o'-lantern glowed from inside a nearby window. The face on the pumpkin seemed to be winking.

The kid in the lead, a hobo, rang the doorbell.

Chuck's heart pounded wildly. His stomach hurt.

Am I nuts? I can't do this!

He imagined himself whirling around, running away.

But before he could move, the inner door opened. A pretty young woman smiled out at them through the screen door, and every kid on the porch chimed out, "Trick or treat!" Musical voices, gruff voices, shy voices, chipper voices. Some seemed to belong to girls, others to boys. Chuck said nothing.

"Trick or treat to you, too," the woman said. Propping the screen door open with her shoulder, she reached into a basket and started giving out small packets of M&Ms. "Here's one for you." She dropped it into the hobo's bag. It made a papery, rattly sound when it landed.

"Thank you," the hobo said. A girl, from the sound of her voice.

"And one for you."

"Thanks."

"Oh, what a pretty princess."

"Thank you."

"And one for you."

After each thump of landing candy, after each thank-you, each kid moved away from the door and Chuck made his way closer. His heart pounded harder, harder. Then he was face to face with the woman. Heart thudding wildly, he smiled and said, "Trick or treat."

"Same to you," she said. Smiling back at him, she dropped two packets of M&M's into his bag. "You get an extra treat for being such a good guy."

He must've looked confused.

"Taking these kids around," she explained. "It's so important that they have an older brother or someone to look after them."

"Well, thanks."

"So dangerous these days. Especially for little kids."

"Yes, it is. Thank you."

"I hope you have a very nice Halloween."

Stunned, he said, "You too."

As she eased the screen door shut, Chuck turned away and hurried after the kids.

They were waiting for him on the sidewalk.

The hobo took a step toward him and blocked his way. The top of her black derby hat was about as high as Chuck's chin. Her face was smudged with soot, probably from a burnt cork. A red bandanna was tied around her neck. She wore a shabby old sports coat with a big white shirt underneath and baggy pants. Resting on her right shoulder was a walking stick with a kerchief bundle dangling from its end. In her left hand, she carried her bag of Halloween candy.

"Hi," Chuck said.

"We don't know you," said the hobo.

A few of the other kids mumbled and nodded.

"I know. I'm—"

"You've been following us."

"Yeah," said a little pirate. Unlike the hobo, he seemed miffed. "How come yer—"

"Knock it off, Ray," the hobo said. Looking up at Chuck, she asked, "You some kinda pervert?" She didn't sound angry, just curious. In the glow of the streetlight, Chuck thought he saw the hint of a smile on her mouth.

"I'm just . . . you know, trick-or-treating."

"By yourself?"

His throat tightened. He nodded. "Yeah. I know I'm too old for it, but . . ."

"How old are you?"

"Fifteen."

"That's pretty old," she said.

"And I'm not exactly wearing a costume."

"Could've fooled me."

Some of the other kids laughed.

"So what's your name?" the hobo asked.

"Chuck."

"Hi, Chuck. I'm Wendy. Three of these ankle-biters are my little brothers and sisters. The rest are friends. So, anyway, you want to come with us?"

Some of the kids made noises of complaint, but none spoke up.

"If it's okay with you," Chuck said.

"We'd be glad to have you with us. Wouldn't we, kids?" There was a hint of threat in her voice.

The kids nodded and mumbled. A few said "Sure," and "Fine," and "Hi."

"Welcome aboard," Wendy told him.

"Thanks. It's really nice of you."

A smile spread over the hobo's grimy face. "We can use a big guy like you to protect us from hoodlums, perverts, and assorted Halloween goblins."

"Great. Thanks."

"By the way," she said, "I'm fifteen, too."

He gaped at her.

"I know, I'm a little small for my age. A pip-squeak. But I'm the same age you are. I guess we probably haven't met because I go to Saint Mary's. The parochial school?"

"Ah."

And so Chuck walked from house to house that Halloween night with Wendy and her group. He said "Trick or treat" with the others, and people in the houses dropped candy into his bag. Nobody complained about his age. Nobody made cracks about his lack of a costume. Apparently, they all assumed, like the first lady had, that he was in charge of this band of cute kids.

Before long, he knew the names of every boy and girl.

He talked with many of them, but mostly he talked with Wendy. And listened to her.

She liked to read. She especially liked scary stories and books. Her favorite television show was "The Twilight Zone."

"Did you know there's a 'Twilight Zone' marathon going on tonight?" Chuck asked.

"I was watching it till about an hour ago." She shrugged. "But you know, it'll be on next year. And Mom and Dad, they've gotta be at some party tonight and they won't let the ankle-biters go trick-or-treating unless I go along, so . . ." She shrugged again. "Here I am." She smiled up at Chuck. "I'm really glad I did take 'em out." As she said that, she leaned sideways and gently bumped against him.

"Me too," he said.

A few minutes later, she said, "Ray, come here." The pirate came over to her. "Want to carry this for me?" She held out her bag of candy.

"Carry your own bag," he said.

"I'll carry it," Chuck offered.

"That would defeat the purpose." To Ray, she said, "Carry it and you can help yourself to a couple of my goodies."

"Yeah? Okay." He took the bag and hurried on ahead.

With her now empty hand, Wendy took hold of Chuck's hand. Smiling up at him, she gave it a squeeze.

He squeezed back, his heart racing.

I must be dreaming, he thought. Or in the Twilight Zone.

The man who opened the door was slim and handsome, perhaps twenty-five or thirty years old. He had short dark hair and a neatly trimmed mustache. He wore a black turtle-neck and black trousers.

"Trick or treat!" the kids yelled.

"Well, well, well," he said. "What have we here?" Standing in the doorway with his back very straight, he smiled and slowly clapped his hands as he studied the group. "Marvelous costumes," he said. "Marvelous. Stand right there while I find you something."

He whirled away and scampered off.

Smiling up at Chuck, Wendy gave his hand a gentle squeeze. "What time do you have to be home?" she whispered.

He shrugged.

"Maybe we can—"

From somewhere deep inside the house came a familiar voice. ". . . not only of sight and sound, but of mind."

"Oh, my God," Chuck muttered.

The man filled the doorway. He now held a silver tray piled with miniature Three Musketeers bars. "Here's one for you," he said and dropped it into Ray's bag.

"Thank you."

"And one for your other bag."

Wendy gave Chuck's hand another squeeze.

"You're watching the 'Twilight Zone' marathon," Chuck said to the man.

"I certainly am. I never miss it."

"Wish I didn't have to miss it."

"You're welcome to come inside and watch it with me. You're all welcome to come in and—"

"We're not allowed to go into strangers' houses," Wendy said.

Chuck met her eyes. "Maybe we could just see one episode . . . ?"

"'All of Us Are Dying,'" the stranger said. "It's just starting."

"That's a really good one," Chuck said. "Maybe . . ."

Wendy shook her head. "No way."

"You could watch it with me," the man said, smiling at Chuck. "They could go on ahead without you."

"I don't know," Chuck muttered, his heart thudding hard.

"This one's a real classic," the man said.

Wendy squeezed Chuck's hand even harder. "I don't think you should, Chuck. *Really.* I mean, no offense, mister, but we don't even know you."

He smiled. "I'm quite harmless."

"Just come with us, Chuck. Okay?"

"'Kick the Can' is next after that," the man said.

Chuck grimaced at Wendy. "I don't know."

"Then comes 'The Howling Man.'"

He started to pull his hand away from Wendy.

She tightened her grip. "Chuck, don't. *Please.*"

Charles Freeman, a boy on the precarious and often frightening edge of manhood, forced into the streets on a Halloween night, finds out that life outside the safety of his home can be more surprising, more gratifying, and yes, more dangerous than an all-night marathon of "The Twilight Zone."

In the Middle of the Night

Edmund Plante

Kelly woke up in the middle of the night, not with a jolt, but with a slow, groggy transition from one world to another. It took a moment to leave behind the former, which quickly fragmented into oblivion, and focus on the reality she'd entered. She thought she had felt a presence. She also thought she had heard breathing – very close. So close that she'd felt heat on her face.

Of course it must have been a dream.

It wasn't like her to wake up at – she glanced at the luminous green digits on the clock on her nightstand – 2:15 in the morning and feel as if someone, *something*, was in the room with her. She quickly clicked on the lamp beside the clock. Although bright light instantly comforted her, told her that she, indeed, was alone in her room, it also brought a sense of shame. When was the last time she'd been afraid of the dark? she asked herself in disgust. When she was a baby, that's when! She was almost seventeen now, jeez!

Yet she found herself reluctant to turn off the lamp. Instead, she decided to get something to drink in the kitchen.

She needed to get up, move around a bit . . . mellow out.

She shrugged into her flannel robe, since it was colder than usual in the house. It had never been like this when only she and her mother lived here. Since Earl, her stepdad and her mother's second husband, had come into their lives about a year ago, they had had to adapt to some changes, and one of the adjustments had been the temperature in the house. Earl had insisted on keeping it cool, had said it was like living in an oven here, and after pointing out that it'd be easier to put on more clothing than to see him take off all of his, Kelly's mother agreed to lower the temperature a few degrees. "Besides, it'll save on fuel," she had told Kelly when Kelly had accused her of being an invertebrate.

Kelly didn't like her stepdad too much, but she didn't hate him either. One thing was certain, though, she was never going to be like her mother. No way would she let any man or boy tell her what to do. She was her own person, independent, even headstrong sometimes — and proud of it!

Walking quietly down the hallway, she paused at her step-brother's room. Jason. Now, he was another adjustment — and a colossal one at that. Unlike his father, Jason made Kelly feel something beyond dislike. She knew "hate" was a strong word, but sometimes she was certain that she indeed did hate him.

There was a strange odor coming from his room. Kelly had caught a whiff of it immediately. She moved closer to the door to define the weird smell. It was tart and dry, a smoky, wood-burning scent with a touch of something else vaguely familiar. Incense? Was that what he'd been doing — burning incense in the middle of the night? The smell was too strong not to be recent. Was this a smell to cover up another smell? she wondered. Like pot?

It wouldn't surprise her if he was smoking drugs. In fact, nothing about him would surprise her. He was a freak, simple as that.

At first, she had felt bad for him. When his mother died two months ago, she had tried to imagine what it would be like if her own mother suddenly died in a car accident too. She found herself unable to imagine it, would probably cry a lake. Jason, however, took it quite well. Too well. He had shown no emotion over his mother's death. He had been like one of those stone-hearted killers who is sentenced to life and shows no trace of remorse on his face. Nothing. At least that was what Kelly's mother had murmured once to herself, a comment Kelly wasn't supposed to hear but did.

After Jason's mother was killed, there was no choice but for his father to take him in. Kelly, her heart breaking for him then, tried to welcome him into the family. He responded by treating her as though she was an inferior high-school freshman and he a superior senior, as though her only purpose was to serve or entertain him. He asked to borrow almost everything she owned: her collection of CDs, money, a school jacket that was her boyfriend's, and her new secondhand car. At first, she had let him have these things. When she stopped letting him borrow her stuff, however (some of the CDs were missing, the money was gone with no promise of payment, the jacket was missing a button and the sleeve was torn at the shoulder, and the car had several cigarette burns on the front seat), he called her a bitch, a slut, and other hateful names.

This wasn't all. The real reason she hated him now was because of what he'd done to her last week. After school, Jason and four of his freaky friends had cornered her in the woods, on a shortcut she usually took every day to and from school. Before that day, she had never been afraid to walk these woods, the distance of which could be covered in less than five minutes if she walked rapidly. She had never had any trouble until these four boys accosted her. (Jason stood apart to watch, saying later with a lazy, sarcastic smirk that since he was half-related to her, it would have been unnatural of him to participate.)

No knives had been pulled out to threaten her, nothing like that. And when she had realized this, she had tried to act tough, pretend they couldn't scare her. But they'd kept closing in on her, closing in until she could feel their bodies as hard as walls pressing against her from all sides. Then she'd felt their hands all over her. She'd felt someone lift the back of her hair and wetly kiss her neck, felt someone lick one side of her face, and felt a hand on her stomach. Panic had exploded inside her and she'd shoved, kicked, and tried to wrench herself free of them. Their bodies had kept pressing, pressing, wouldn't stop, so she'd screamed as loud as she could. She hadn't been very far from the main road; she'd thought someone would certainly hear her.

This had worked, the scream. The guys had run. Only Jason had remained, and he'd laughed quietly. It was at that moment, as she'd watched him chuckle, rolling a toothpick from one side of his mouth to the other, that she'd known she truly hated him. She had wanted to lash out at him but didn't. Instead, she'd tried to show him that he hadn't frightened her as much as he'd thought. She'd coolly given him the finger, then turned her back on him and continued as calmly as she could toward home.

When she was safely in her room with the door locked, she hadn't been able to stop shivering. What would have happened if she hadn't screamed? she'd wondered. How far would Jason's friends have gone while he watched? Why was

Jason so . . . so mean? What had she ever done for him to treat her like this?

Her mother and his father had changed since Jason moved into the house, she realized. Strict rules had been laid out for him: he had a curfew; he had chores to do around the house; he had to keep up his school grades; and most of all, he had to stop swearing, especially around his father and stepmother. At first, Jason ignored these rules. Loud, ugly arguments and threats ensued. He was grounded, and for a while it seemed Jason was finally under parental control.

Then everything changed, to Kelly's puzzlement. Now Jason seemed to be controlling *them*. He came home whenever he damned please, did absolutely nothing around the house, and swore like a drunk. It was as if they'd actually grown afraid of him. Kelly couldn't understand what had caused this sudden reversal, but there was one thing she was sure of — she wasn't going to let Jason control her, *ever*. She wasn't afraid of him.

Now she turned away from her stepbrother's door and continued toward the kitchen. As she entered the room, she flipped on the ceiling light and helped herself to a small bottle of mineral water from the refrigerator. As she took a sip, she became aware of the silence. It seemed magnified and unnatural, probably because of the late hour. She felt almost as if she were doing something illegal, being up and about in the middle of the night like this while the rest of the house was sleeping.

Having decided to take the water with her, she began to head back to her room. She stopped when she noticed that the door to the cellar was ajar. Automatically, she blamed Jason. He was always down there in the cellar, and he was always forgetting to close this door when he came back up. He had set up a little band down there, he and his buddies, although Kelly never heard them play all that much. She suspected that Jason and his friends did other things, drugs and alcohol maybe.

She was moving toward the door to close it when she caught a whiff of that strange sharp, smoky smell again, that same odor that had come from Jason's room. She leaned forward into the darkness beyond the door. The smell was stronger. It definitely was coming from the cellar below.

For a long moment she stood on the top step, debating whether to descend. She thought of all the movies she'd seen where the heroines stupidly search dark, creepy places to locate a noise. How many times had she laughed at these girls or women and called them morons? So why was she thinking of doing the same thing right now?

For one thing, she reminded herself, it would not be the noise she would be locating – it would be the smell. And for another thing, what if the odor was something dangerous, like gas leaking from the furnace down there? She should check it out and then alert her mother and Earl, shouldn't she?

Yet she hesitated. She flipped the switch at the top of the stairs and saw the light come on below. She stared at the illuminated cellar, still hesitating.

What was she afraid of?

The furnace was near the bottom of the stairs. She wouldn't need to cross the entire cellar. And it was well lit.

Having at last convinced herself that there was nothing to be afraid of, that it was very important to check out the strange odor, and that she would not be doing what those dumb heroines did in movies, she began her descent into the cellar.

It was very warm at the bottom. The smell was strong down here too, seemingly making the air thick and dusty. But the smell wasn't coming from the direction of the furnace, Kelly realized. It seemed strongest in the opposite area, where there was a door that led to a smaller, inner cellar where her mother stored her garden tools and clay flowerpots.

Without letting herself think about what she was doing, Kelly headed for the door, which was nothing more than a flimsy see-through gate made of splintered boards and chicken wire. As she pulled on the rusty thumb-latch handle, she noticed that some of her mother's tools and flowerpots had been removed from this smaller cellar and stashed in a heap in a shadowy area not too far outside the door. When did her mother do this? Or rather, *why* did she do this? Kelly knew her mother was usually peculiar in keeping all her things in their proper places. She was orderly to a fault. This wasn't something she would do. Someone else must have done this. Jason?

Kelly groped for the pull-string to the light somewhere above the door. After what seemed like a century, she found it and yanked. Nothing happened. She pulled at the string once more, and again accomplished only a dead click. Obviously, the light bulb had burnt out or was missing.

But her eyes had already begun to adjust to the gloom ahead of her. The light from the outer cellar behind her also aided her, and she could see black bulks and objects here and there, although, as had happened before in her room, she could not readily define the shapes in shadows.

The smell in here was almost choking. All the moisture seemed to have been sucked out of the air. She was now reminded of a stench from her chemistry class. Sulfur.

And it was much warmer in here, almost as if a bonfire were raging nearby. She could actually feel heat on her face.

Why? Where was the heat coming from? She could see only darkness . . . and darker shapes. No hint of fire.

She thought of leaving, told herself she didn't need to know what was in here, what was causing the overpowering smell and inexplicable heat. Yet she found herself moving deeper into the room.

She paused before what seemed to be a wooden table. Her hands carefully explored its surface. Her fingers touched sticky liquid, and she quickly pulled away, repulsed. As she stepped back in haste, her foot hit something, knocking it aside.

Curious, she dropped to her knees and groped in search of the object. When she located it, she gingerly let her fingers explore its shape. It was cylindrical, about five inches high and three inches wide. Most of it was hard, smooth, and cool to the touch, but she was surprised to find that a portion at the top was soft, lumpy, and quite warm. Using both hands, she picked it up and brought it closer to her face to better examine it. She recognized the smell of wax at once. Warm wax. She now realized that she was holding not only a fat, barrel-shaped candle, but also a candle that had been burning very recently.

As though suddenly afraid that it was a time bomb she was holding, Kelly immediately set the candle back down on the dirt floor. That was when she noticed there were other black cylinder-shaped objects on the floor – candles. There were at least six of them. Why? What was their purpose?

Despite the room's parched heat, Kelly's insides went cold. The candles were arranged in a circle as if . . .

Kelly hurried back out to the first cellar, to the light. For a fleeting instant, she was flooded with relief – like a child who has just reached the safety post in a children's game – until she noticed that some of her fingertips were smeared red. Paint? Blood? She remembered she'd touched something sticky on the table (altar?) in the other cellar.

She didn't know how long she had been staring at her fingers, her mind grappling to understand, when she heard what she first thought was a soft rumble behind her. It wasn't until she heard it a second time that she realized it was actually a growl.

Although it was barely audible, it felt close. *Very* close.

Kelly's heart pounded in her chest. She couldn't bring herself to turn around to look. She heard the growl a third time; it was lower, deeper, and conjured up an image of a crouching dog baring its teeth and readying to pounce.

At last the paralysis broke and she bolted like an arrow from a bow for the stairs. She didn't stop until she was in her room, the door locked behind her.

Back in her bed, she began to wonder if she had imagined the growl. When she remembered the blood – or whatever it was – on her fingers, she put her hand under the bedside lamp to examine them. The dark, smeared stains were still there. She desperately wanted to wash her hand, but there was no way she was going to leave her room now.

She listened to assure herself that whoever or whatever had growled wasn't outside her door. Only her own breathing disrupted what otherwise would have been complete silence. She slid deeper beneath the covers.

Her mind raced. Should she tell her mother what she had discovered tonight? And exactly what was that? That Jason was practicing witchcraft, black magic, something like this? What other explanation was there for the circle of candles and blood on a table, which had to be some kind of sacrificial altar? And then there was the overwhelming smell of . . . brimstone? This smell was clinging to her now, as if she'd spent hours in a crowded room with cigarette smokers. This explained why she had smelled this odor coming from Jason's room; he had been down in that small cellar room tonight, probably only minutes before her.

Yes, she would tell her mother in the morning. Would she believe her? As she wondered about this, she was reminded once again that her mother's and Earl's behavior toward Jason had changed recently. Was this because they had already discovered what Jason was doing and were now afraid of him?

Well, this isn't going to happen to me! Kelly vowed. She didn't care what he did in that cellar. She didn't even care if he had conjured up Satan himself. She was not going to let him control her the way he was controlling her mother and his father. There was no way she was going to let him intimidate her! *No way!*

She wasn't sure if she fell back to sleep, but the next time she looked at her clock it was 4:16. Although morning would soon break, it was darker than ever. She knew she wouldn't even see her hand if she brought it close to her face.

But she did see something. It was not a dark, obscure bulk as before, but a glimmer of greenish yellow light. Actually, there were two points of light, like a set of eyes watching her from not too far away. She wasn't sure – maybe it was her imagination again – but the twin points of light seemed to be moving very slowly toward her.

Kelly closed her eyes and told herself the glowing "eyes" would be gone the next time she looked.

They weren't. And now she saw a face accompanying the eyes, a face that was vaguely visible below its eyes' eerie glow. And it was a familiar face.

As Kelly's frantic mind tried to place the face, another set of burning eyes appeared in another part of the room. And another. These, too, floated almost imperceptibly toward her bed. When they were all around her, close enough for her to see what she could of their ghostly faces, she gasped with recognition.

These were Jason's four friends, the guys who had tried to force themselves on her that day in the woods. But these boys weren't real, she desperately told herself. Their eyes were too bright, too filled with unnatural, demonic light. This was a hallucination. Or a dream. Yes, she was dreaming.

Yet she could feel their hands on her. As had happened in the woods, she felt their bodies pushing against her, felt their hands slithering over her body, felt their lips and their cold, wet tongues lick her cheeks, lips, and neck.

Go away! she mentally screamed. Go away! This is only a dream! A dream!

But they wouldn't go away. She lashed out, kicked and thrashed, but couldn't connect with anything solid. The boys were apparitions, definitely hallucinations, yet their bodies and their hands and their incredibly cold, wet mouths felt so real. Remotely, she remembered reading something about astral projections and out-of-body experiences. Was this what was happening? Were these friends of Jason's doing this right now, their spiritual selves here while their physical bodies were home? Or was it only her mind that was being manipulated, being tricked from a distance into seeing things that weren't really happening?

Jason was responsible for this! Of this she was certain. He was doing this because he wanted to control her with fear, just as he could now control the rest of his new family.

She felt an icy, clammy hand slip beneath her nightshirt. Its touch was as jolting as ocean water. The hand began to slither upward. More fingers grasped one of her legs and crawled like icy worms up her thigh.

This time she screamed out loud. "Get off! Get off! Off!"

All at once they were gone. But it was not her screams that did it, she realized as she bolted upright in bed – it was her mother pounding at the locked door, shouting, "Kelly! Kelly! Are you all right in there?"

Kelly found herself briefly disoriented and stunned, as though she had just stepped off a dizzying carnival ride. She needed a moment to compose herself.

God, what a horrible dream.

And it was a dream, of course. Wasn't it?

"Kelly, answer me!" her mother demanded.

After clicking on the bedside lamp, Kelly unlocked the door.

"My God, you sounded like you were being murdered in there!" her mother cried, although she seemed relieved when it became apparent that Kelly was okay.

"I . . . I had an awful nightmare."

"Are you okay now, sweetheart?"

"Yes, Mom. I'm okay now."

Her mother regarded her for a moment, touched her face affectionately, then whispered, "Well, then, good night," as she kissed Kelly's cheek.

After her mother was gone, Kelly returned to bed. She turned off the light. The whole thing was a dream, she told herself again. Even what she'd found in the cellar, the circle of candles, the blood, the whole thing. A very bad dream.

When she woke up again, it was to bright morning sunlight. What had happened in the middle of the night was vivid in her mind. It was not vague, and it did not dissipate like smoke as most dreams did. But it *had* been a dream, she staunchly told herself. Yes. A dream.

In the kitchen, she found Jason eating his usual breakfast of Devil Dog and chocolate milk. His father and her mother had tried to stop him from eating such junk food for breakfast. In the beginning they had succeeded,

Kelly remembered. But now he ate whatever he wanted.

"Hey, there," he greeted around a mouthful of food when he spotted Kelly. "I was wondering when you were going to get up."

"Why?" she asked warily. She saw there was something around his neck, something she hadn't noticed before.

"Okay if I borrow your car? Me and my buddies want to, you know, like, ride around a bit after school."

It was a silver chain on his neck, and there was what looked like a crucifix dangling from it.

"Hey, you deaf?" he asked impatiently when she didn't answer.

"I heard you."

"Well, then?"

The crucifix was upside down.

"No. I already told you, you can't—" She couldn't finish, for she felt a strange flash of pain behind one eye. He was staring hard at her, grinning faintly now. She looked away, as though his gaze was literally penetrating, worming deeply into her brain, seizing it. She looked again at the inverted crucifix.

"Well, then?" she heard him repeat.

She swallowed. "Yeah, sure," she said. "You can . . . you can borrow it anytime you want."

Old One/New One

Nancy Kilpatrick

Cass flicked on her disposable lighter to gaze into the polished metal. Gram had insisted that the ancient art of scrying with a copper mirror was necessary for coaxing back spirits. Cass wasn't convinced. After all, her grandmother didn't know everything, although she'd always acted as if she did.

The full moon was bright enough that together with the little flame, Cass could clearly see her purple nightshade eyes, the same color as Gram's. And her raven hair – the color Gram's must have been when she was a girl, before she turned all white. "This world's pure illusion. Copper reveals the truth." Gram had told her that, and a lot of other things.

The trees stood like sentries protecting the sacred round. Walking barefoot at night through century-old spruce and white ash hadn't been Cass's idea of a fun evening. Bloody scratches painted her face and arms, not to mention the soles of her feet. But that's what Gram had instructed, and Cass had given her word.

Gram had called her here, just like she'd said she would. Almost a year had passed since her grandmother's death, so Cass had been expecting something. The dream came last night. Tonight was All Hallows Eve, the time when the spirits of the departed crack the seam separating realities and come back to speak with the living.

Cass spread a blanket over the mound of poison ivy and built a small fire. She should have got here at sunset. Well, she was late. She'd had to finish up a paper for school and do her laundry. . . . It would have to do. Gram wouldn't approve, but then there were many things Cass had done of which Gram hadn't approved.

When Cass was a child, she had tried to please her grandmother. But the older she got, the less possible that seemed. She'd had to find her own ground, at least that's how it was from her end. Gram, of course, had seen things differently.

The full moon needed time to scale the sky. It was too early to start the potion, but the chilly night made her want something warm to drink. She half filled the sooty pot with water she'd lugged from the pond beside the cottage. Gram had instructed her where to find the white-spotted red mushroom, and how to slice it thinly and make tea. Cass was glad she'd spent the last year reading, delving into all the chemistry books she could get her hands on. She loved chemistry especially, and easily discovered that belladonna neutralizes the poisonous effects of fly agaric while enhancing its hallucinogenic qualities. She'd brought some along and tossed the leaves of the "beautiful woman" into the pot, followed by a handful each of devil's claw and sassafras; it wouldn't hurt to dim the bitterness of this tea.

The mixture steeped for what felt like a long time. It wasn't nearly ready, but she scooped some into a clay bowl anyway, telling herself she'd drink more later. The tea was still bitter. She remembered the taste from when she'd drunk it with her grandmother. She'd been just a kid, maybe seven, and thought she'd die. After that summer, Cass had seen things differently.

"Fly agaric," Gram laughed. "We'll fly to the moon, you and I. Then we'll see what an old crone like me can do with a fresh life before she passes to the beyond."

"Gram, don't leave me!"

"Learn your lessons well, child, and your gram will not have to leave you."

"I'll study, Gram, really hard. So you don't have to die."

"Die? Who said anything about dying? Of course you'll learn. You're so very like me. But a lazy child. That will change."

But it hadn't changed. Cass knew she was still lazy, at least by Gram's standards. She never studied enough or learned fast enough, and she always took shortcuts, and, and, and . . . Like the fasting. Gram told her in the dream to drink only water today, but she'd substituted fruit juice at breakfast and had half a pita with cheese and tomato for lunch. It wasn't much. It couldn't hurt. She'd seen Gram substitute or change things all the time and the spells still worked.

This night was alive. Silvery branches extended toward her like arms. She noticed knots in the trunks of the deciduous trees and recognized them for what they were: spirits living in the bark. If she asked, and if they were in a generous mood, they might reveal knowledge, of primal energies, of the forces of life and death. And Gram was near. Waiting. Cass felt that to her marrow.

The tea warmed Cass, although it made her stomach hurt a little. Above, the full moon filled the sky, casting light just for her.

Cass was eight years old when her mother and father decided that seeing Gram wasn't such a good idea. When her dad died two years later of a sudden heart attack, her mom let her visit Gram in the summer again. She'd always had the feeling, though, that her mother was never completely comfortable with the idea of those visits. Once, Mom's sister, Aunt Sylvia, a quiet, serious woman, said that seeing Gram wasn't healthy. A month or so later, Aunt Sylvia died in a car accident. After the funeral, Cass's mother never quite recovered, and Cass went to live with Gram.

Cass looked around the clearing, two miles from her grandmother's cottage. She had spent fifteen summers in these isolated woods. Now she owned the land, and the cottage. Forever. Her roots were planted here. Her gram lingered in every leaf and insect. Riding the elementals. Communing with the Queen of Shades.

Tonight Cass would talk with her grandmother again, learning the secrets there hadn't been time to learn before. Asking the questions that she had been forbidden to ask – about her powers, and her destiny.

A great horned owl hooted. The melancholy sound coated the night air. The thought came to Cass that something from this night would not exist in the morning! She picked up the copper mirror with the crossed handle – the sign of Venus. Its creamy surface reflected eyes so much like Gram's. Widely set, dreamy, one more purple than the other, irises flecked with darkness.

Cass gathered fist-sized limestone rocks and placed them around the edge of the circle of firelight, creating a barrier from the shadows beyond, careful to leave one space open. An entrance. Lime, she recalled from her reading, came from limestone – rock that had been formed from sediments, predominantly calcium carbonate. Gram had never wanted her to know things like that. In her hands, Cass felt the power of the skeletons of the marine micro-organisms that had given their lives so that this rock could be formed. They had dwelled here before the ice age, before this land was buried beneath glaciers. Gram had told her to bring shale from the cottage because of the clay content, the clay from which all flesh is born. But why pack that weight when the limestone was nearby? Besides, the remains of these ancient life forms gave Cass a sense of her own strength and history, of her destiny. She was convinced she had lived many lifetimes, as many as her Gram had, and would continue into the future.

Her movements must have activated particular properties of the fly agaric. She picked up a rock, or at least she thought she had, but a second later her hands were empty.

When the circle was complete, Cass used Gram's athame to consecrate the ground. She stood in the center of the circle and pointed the tip of the bone-handled ceremonial knife at the rocks, moving counter-clockwise. "*Echo echo azarak, echo echo zamarak.*" She had forgotten the sage stick and had to purify the interior by burning pine needles, which, she'd read, many cultures have used to purify space. Pine would work just as well, and it was indigenous to the area — sage was not. Surely Gram would not find fault with that! From the black velvet pouch she wore around her neck, she took ten crystals and arranged them. Clear and hematite — white and black — to the north. More opposites — rose quartz and red jasper, lapis lazuli and blue lace agate — to the south. The malachite and botswana she placed at the west for finality. The yellow tiger's eye and yellow onyx at the east, where the stone was missing. Where the sun rises. An invitation to the other world.

Cass had selected the dried herbs and roots and seeds and other things she'd been instructed in the dream to use this night from the hundreds of glass and porcelain jars that lined the shelves in her grandmother's cottage. She hoped she hadn't missed any – writing on the labels had worn away, and in some cases, she'd had to trust her sense of smell.

"Writing! That's how they learned our powers and stole them!" Gram snapped at the mere suggestion of books, and alluded to the burning times, when witches had almost become extinct. *"But we came back,"* she said, *"and will again. And again. My power will be yours, and then yours will rebuild mine."*

Cass was thirteen when her gram had said that last bit, and she wasn't sure just what she meant. She knew only that Gram promised never to leave her alone in a world that does not understand you when you're different. And now she was alone, here in the woods. Until Gram came back.

There was still time – the moon hadn't reached its zenith. Cass's stomach began to cramp. To distract herself, she shuffled the tarot deck, laying out the medieval cards in the Celtic pattern. As she turned over the four cards that predicted her future, she was surprised to see Death. A foreboding. She *had* altered parts of the ritual. Maybe it wouldn't work properly. Maybe something awful would happen. Maybe Gram was right about her. Maybe . . .

But the belladonna kicked in and eradicated the physical discomfort and uneasy thoughts. When Cass had started college last fall, she'd moved into residence, away from her mom. An ending is a small death, she reminded herself, and then felt better.

On her deathbed, Gram had asked Cass never to abandon this land. She'd tried to exact a promise. The most Cass would swear to, however, was that she would come back this night and perform the ceremony her gram requested.

But for the past eight months, she'd found herself digging into physics and chemistry texts while she continued practicing the spells Gram had taught her. Most spells were simple, alchemical in nature, but not all could be explained away by logic. The conjurings increased in complexity as time passed. Just last month, she was able to transform matter. She hatched a fertile goose egg using just her hands, and cooked another one the same way. It was a major breakthrough. That night she had a dream.

Gram was livid. Once again, Cass had not gone about things in the right way. "Idle hands and child's play! Indolent girl! Wasting time while the wheel spins — life, death, rebirth. You have a higher purpose. One day you'll regret those squandered hours. Remember, when I call you, you must come to me!"

Whether Cass had been right or wrong, each step of her existence seemed to have led to this night. This must be the night of her initiation, when the powers she possessed would blossom into sacred knowledge, when she would come fully into her own. The night she would bring Gram back for a chat.

A somber cloud swallowed the moon. When the Mistress of the Night disappeared, Cass used her light to stare in the copper mirror. A wrinkled face surrounded the eyes. She blinked and the wrinkles evaporated. Her gram had insisted that the eyes are not windows to the soul, as everybody thinks, but doorways through which souls pass. As Cass focused on the large black dots at the center, she saw something there.

Wind rushed through the trees and surrounded her. Chilly fingers slid up the insides of her bare legs. She wrapped Gram's heavy shawl tighter around her naked shoulders and tossed a handful of ground black coriander and day lily tubers into the transforming fire. Sparks leapt at the air spirits, who snuffed them in their fists. The trees had moved closer to the circle, seeking warmth and protection.

Cass opened the large leather bag she had brought along. She unwrapped the black silk fabric with the silver pentacle painted in the center and placed the clear glass pillbox on top.

Cass opened the lid. Inside lay fifty strands of her grand-mother's snow white hair, cut just before she died. She picked up the athame and cut a lock of her own dark hair. Rather than tediously counting out fifty strands, she estimated. She laid her hair with Gram's in one palm and rubbed them together so that the strands mingled. Then she offered them to the moon with a chant praising the beauty of her celestial mistress.

Tonight the moon showed two faces – Cass had never noticed before. It must be an omen. The light face, what she'd imagined in her naivete to be the whole, could obviously not function without the larger, darker visage. The symbiotic twins reminded her of her own face and her grandmother's. Similar but different. Gram must have looked like her when she was a girl. She would look like Gram when she aged.

Cass rocked to the comforting chant she mumbled. Eventually, she became aware that she had been rocking and chanting a long time. Overhead, the moon shone brilliant until a cloud cut across it, turning that fullness into a silver scythe, a blade that had moved dangerously close.

She must hurry, but she felt too dizzy to stand. From where she sat, she threw the hairs at the fire. Flames singed most of them, but some missed their mark and landed on the ground. What could she do about it now?

The copper mirror reflected only pupils. Darkness had devoured the irises. By the blazing light of the moon and fire, the image in her eyes twisted and writhed, furious to escape. It seemed to expand even as she watched. "Gram, is that you?" The air stilled as the temperature plummeted. Cass's heart cried in her ears. She could run into the forest and demand protection from the spirits there, but she'd be letting Gram down. And she had sworn an oath. Gram had taken her in when there was no one else. All her life, she had relied on her grandmother. Now Gram was relying on her. Suddenly, she felt terrified. What if she had botched things? Had selected the wrong herbs? Or what if the moon was now too high in the sky? Or if instead of calling Gram, she had summoned another soul? Or summoned something *without* a soul, something not quite of this universe?

There was nothing to do but look again. The darkness in her pupils sprang forward. Cass jumped back. If it was Gram, why didn't she answer?

Trembling, Cass held the copper over the steaming cauldron to clear the surface. She could not feel the fire's heat on her skin. Darkness loomed at the doorway, waiting for the chant her gram had demanded she memorize until it was embedded in every cell. She remembered the shame as her grandmother's words came back to haunt her: *"Your light burns bright as mine dims. I need a spark. Just a spark. You'll do that for your gram, won't you?"*

"But, Gram, what if I make a mistake?"

"Nonsense, lazy child! You will not make a mistake! Recite it again. Now. And again. And again. Until you become the words."

Cass's voice trembled as she whispered: "Old one/new one. Now! Both of you."

The ground beneath her rumbled. Could this be an earthquake? She gazed into the copper and no longer saw herself. The dark creature sprinted. Frantic and powerful, it popped out of her black pupils like a baby being born. The earth she sat on split open, throwing her onto her back. In the distance she heard a howl.

"Old one/new one. Now! Both of you."

Fire and moon, fire and ice. The swarthy creature swallowed both. Enough light was left to see the gnarled shape shift into something unrecognizable. Where the ground had cracked, a cavity formed. Within it lay Gram's corpse. Cold and still as limestone. It bolted upright and, grinning, opened its legs and arms. Cass pulled back.

"Come to me, child. Now! I'm counting on you."

Lightning shattered the obsidian sky. Electricity charged Cass's body. The circle swelled with a kinetic presence. She moved the athame to nudge the last limestone rock into place, trapping herself with the energy, as if sealing a dead body in a tomb. The moment the circle closed, the down-pour hit.

A wall of icy liquid dropped on her. She knew she must be chilled, but she felt nothing. She squatted and looked down into the pit at her grandmother's rotting bones and saw her own knees trembling in terror.

"Old one/new one. Now! Both of you." Her voice sounded strangely tinny. The dark entity trapped within the circle with her coalesced at the head of the grave. Cass stared into the face of dissolution. Voluptuous and lecherous, the vile energy reached out and fondled her. From below, brittle fin-gerbones dug between her ribs, pulling her down, searching for her heart.

"Gram?" Cass screamed. "Where are you?" This was not how it was suppose to go. Gram was supposed to come and *talk* with her, only talk. This alien force wanted more. It was hungry. It wanted to possess her body and eat her soul.

Thunder roared and lightning struck a tree close by. The seam binding reality split. In that moment, the Queen of the Dead, garbed in malevolence, beckoned. Cass understood. If she did not follow willingly, she would be dragged away against her will.

Her head fell back. Lightning illuminated the sky. The moon split in two. Its parts formed eyes holding essential truths that burned into her cells.

Cass wrenched herself out of the dark embrace and hurtled her body forward, kicking a stone away, breaking the circle. Somehow she had the presence of mind to grab the athame and shove the stone back into place, closing the door.

Outside the round she was vulnerable to elementals and wandering spirits, but she prayed she would be safe from what had been lured inside.

The ominous energy raged and the skeletal remains became animate. Their lascivious *danse macabre* promised annihilation. A murmur clung to her, deadly as a black widow's kiss. *Old one/new one. Now! Both of you.* The words vibrated, and she clamped a hand over her mouth to keep from joining in. Consciousness flooded her: this was a test! Her own hand could have opened the world to infinite darkness!

Cass collapsed onto the earth's moist bosom. She offered anguished wails and eternal sobs. Tears and rain fell, and the earth shook until the pieces of the moon finally dropped into the abyss.

With daylight came sounds.

Birdsong.

Rain dripped from leaf to leaf to ground.

Warm air thawed chilled flesh.

Cass's body trembled violently as she stood on legs that barely held her. The limestone had melted to pebbles, the soil surrounding them was whitewashed.

She stepped into the circle. The mound of Gram's grave was alive with insects and white lily of the valley, as fresh as Cass had found it. Where the pot had overturned, the toxic tea had mixed with the mud. The athame blade and handle had separated. She dug through the soil to find her crystals but could not locate the transformers, the yellow onyx and the tiger's eye. Most of the tarot cards were dirty but intact. Death, though, had been badly stained by the lime, which was already eating through the thick paper about the skeleton's ribs. Where its heart would have been.

Of all her precious ritual objects, only the copper mirror remained completely unscathed. Cass peered in. A shock of white hair covered her head. Brilliant sunshine on metal reflected light and dark amethyst irises and shrank the black pupils to pinpoints.

As she pocketed the mirror and the pebble that had functioned as the door, Cass whispered a thanks to her grandmother for this new lesson, which had revealed the scope of her powers. And the viciousness of Gram's intentions. Those micro-organisms may have altered, but they were still around. So was she. Gram wasn't. That, too, is the way the wheel spins.

Hell-Bent for Leather

Michael Kelly

Who knew it would be so dark? Otis thought. So dark and so wet. He should have brought a flashlight, but then he remembered it was against *the rules*.

Lightning flashed, and the wind and pouring rain stung him. Out of the corner of his eye, Otis saw movement. Someone was hiding behind that tombstone over there. One of the gang, he knew. One of the Tuxedo Boys. Named for their penchant of wearing black. A black leather jacket with a crisp white T-shirt beneath it.

They were just trying to spook him, is all. Outside the graveyard, before he'd scrabbled spider-like over the wall, they'd told him about the Shambler. Simon, his face dead serious, had whispered softly in his ear about a man seen roaming the graveyard each Halloween. A man with a knife, his gray-green flesh hanging in tatters from gleaming bone. A restless soul, shuffling slowly amid the cenotaphs and gravestones of the dank, misty cemetery. The rest of the Tuxedo Boys hadn't met his eyes. They had just stood around, hands shoved deep in their pockets, foggy breath steaming from their mouths, idly kicking at the ground like nervous, impatient stallions.

Yeah, thought Otis, just trying to scare me. Just trying to put the fear in me. He shivered, pulled his hands from his pockets, and wrapped his arms around himself for some warmth and comfort. His long, dirty blond hair hung wet and limp. His feet pulled free of the mud with a sucking sound, and he realized he was standing on a freshly turned grave.

Boom!

What was that? Easy now, Otis, he thought. Just a bit of thunder, not a tomb door slamming shut.

Christ, he thought. Halloween, All Hallows Eve, and I'm slinking around a cemetery to earn my leather jacket. It seemed simple enough at the time, but now he just wanted to get it over with and get the hell out of there.

He remembered last week, at Old Man McCutcheon's farm, when Simon had earned *his* jacket. The Tuxedo Boys had let him tag along, a kind of pre-initiation. Simon had hidden on the porch, a large jack-o'-lantern with the bottom cut out nestled in the crook of his arm. They'd flushed McCutcheon out of his big old house by throwing crab apples through his windows. Apples off the same trees that McCutcheon, yelling and shaking his wooden cane, had chased Otis from each summer for as far back as he could recall.

I'll get you for this, Otis Travers. You'll burn in hell, laddie.

Sure enough, McCutcheon had come shambling out of his house onto the porch, leaning on his cane, all hunched over and wheezing like a leaky radiator. He tottered forward, his old bones creaking loudly and his fist shaking in the air.

"Is that you, little Otis Travers?"

Little. Otis had bristled at the word. Little. What would the others think? Always little. Wee, little Otis. Each and every year, the smallest kid in class. The runt of the litter.

Then Old Man McCutcheon had lifted the hickory cane and waved it feebly in the cool night air. It had reminded Otis of a birthday party he'd attended a few years back, where each child was blindfolded, given a stick, and told to take a few whacks at the swinging piñata. McCutcheon had looked like an enraged and sullen child, always missing his target, more frantic with each swing. "You'll burn, I tell you."

And then Simon had plopped the pumpkin on McCutcheon's head. The old man had dropped his cane, both hands at the sides of the pumpkin, trying to force it from his head. "You'll burn in hell for this! Burn in hell!" came the muffled voice.

That's when Otis had stepped forward and shoved McCutcheon.

McCutcheon had reeled on the porch, arms windmilling for balance, then toppled down the three short steps. His pumpkin head had hit the step post with a dull thud and cracked open, smearing the walkway in a pulpy, stringy pumpkin gore. The old man's body had trembled, and a wheezy, phlegmy rattle had issued from his mouth. Then he had lain still.

Christ, Otis had thought. He hadn't meant to hurt the old bastard. Just scare him a bit, get the old man back for calling him little.

The Tuxedo Boys had stood around the limp form, Simon prodding the body with a black-booted foot, testing for movement.

"Is he dead?" Otis had stammered.

Simon had been slow to answer, his face all screwed up, looking both scared and scary, a peculiar sparkle coming from his dark eyes. When he'd finally spoken, it was whisper soft. "I don't know. Is he breathing?"

Otis had tugged at Simon's shiny black leather sleeve. "We gotta call an ambulance, or the cops."

"No!" Simon had said. "No cops." He had turned, looked at Otis. "You wanna go to jail?"

"N-no."

"Neither do I. Not for this. Maybe we could call an ambulance. See if he's breathing."

Shaking, Otis had crouched down beside McCutcheon's lumpy form, peered into his dull face.

At that moment, McCutcheon's eyes had sprung open, black anger clouding them, and the old man's hand had shot out and grabbed hold of Otis's shirt. McCutcheon, mouth agape, had pulled Otis close, his foul, fetid breath washing over Otis in a sick wave. Otis had backpedaled, struggled to break free from McCutcheon's claw-like grip. He'd twisted around, nearly pulling McCutcheon off the ground, then broken loose, leaving the old man sputtering angrily on the walkway.

Otis and the others had bolted like balls on a billiard table, scattering in all directions. Glancing back, he'd seen McCutcheon peeling the broken pumpkin from his head, had seen his mouth moving and heard the wind carrying the words to him.

"Going to get you, Otis. Get you for this."

Otis shivered at the memory, shook his head. Midnight. Just got to hang in there till midnight, he thought.

But what if he left now? Who would know?

They'd know, he thought. He couldn't see them, but he knew they were there somewhere. Probably still outside the high, black, wrought-iron gates. He could picture them – the Tuxedo Boys – all black leather and orange cigarette glows under sodium streetlights, grinning darkly at his expense.

And of course, there was the one in the cemetery with him. Probably Simon. Crazy Simon, the practical joker.

No, he'd have to wait it out. Oh, and push over a headstone. That was part of the deal.

Otis glanced about in the dark for a small gravestone. He spied one a few plots over, and trudged through the rain and the wind and the cemetery dirt. Bending, Otis shoved against the stone, feet straining for traction on the mudslicked ground. Otis grunted and pushed. The headstone toppled over, landing with a dull, liquid splat. Not unlike the sound Old Man McCutcheon's head had made when it struck the post.

Ha! he thought, that wasn't so tough. I'll show them. Otis tramped along the row of stones, toppling the ones he could, kicking and spitting at the ones he couldn't. At the end of the row, he turned and surveyed the damage. Not bad, he thought, rubbing his hands together.

A brief crackle of lightning illuminated the graveyard. A dark figure was lumbering toward Otis, the wind whipping the tattered rags it wore. Otis smiled. C'mon, Simon, or whoever you are, give us your best shot.

Otis envisioned slipping his arms into the shiny, crow black leather jacket, roaming the shadowy night-drenched streets with the Tuxedo Boys, and he trembled in anticipation. He remembered leaving the house, and his mom calling after him: "Otis, my little one, don't be getting up to no mischief, you hear? And don't be chasing round with them Tuxedo Boys. They'll be the death of you." He'd smirked at that and slammed the door shut behind him.

Little, she'd called him. *My little one.* Well, he'd show her who was little. Just like he'd shown that old geezer McCutcheon. *Is that you, little Otis Travers?* An angry sigh escaped Otis's lips, hanging for a moment in the still night air, then scuttling away like dead October leaves in grimy street gutters. Who's little now? he thought.

Through rain-blurred eyes, Otis saw the silent black shape ambling toward him. It was closer now. Much closer. Something glinted in its right hand. The wind whispered *Otis-s-s-s* . . . The sound was like fingernails scraped along a chalkboard, and he chuckled nervously because he knew the wind couldn't speak. He must be hearing things.

And Otis trembled again. "Sheesh, Simon, that's a good one. Went all out for Halloween, didn't ya?"

Otis turned and ran, laughing. "C'mon, Simon. Catch me if you can."

Otis slipped, fell in the mud. He turned over onto his back. Simon was still coming on, steady as the rain. Otis saw the knife clearly this time. It was long and curved and gleamed sharply in a brief flicker of lightning. And Simon's head was a grinning, glowing pumpkin head.

"Y-yeah, okay, Simon. You can stop now."

The Simon thing shuffled forward, knife raised high.

"C'mon, Simon. You're scaring me."

And the blade inched higher, the pumpkin grin grew wider, a hoarse wail issuing from the black, moist maw.

"You'll burn, little Otis-s-s-s . . ."

"That's enough now!"

Otis quivered, scrambled to his feet and ran for the gate, glancing back at the Simon thing tracking him through the dark, wet cemetery. He fell again, got up, dared a look over his shoulder, and an icy wave of fear coursed through him. The Simon thing was a few feet away, the knife swooshing through the air. The smell of worms and rotted pumpkins assailed him.

Turning, Otis again ran. He could see small, dark forms on the other side of the gate. They appeared to be shouting and waving. As he got closer, he saw them: the Tuxedo Boys, including – dear God Almighty – Simon!

And he heard them, as well: "Get out! Get out! For Chrissakes, Otis, get the hell out!"

His heart pounding, Otis raced for the gate. Then, suddenly, the ground dropped away and he landed heavily, face down in thick mud, his head striking an exposed rock. Dazed, he slowly rolled over and stared up through the red cloud of blood running into his eyes. He was six feet down, looking up from a newly dug grave.

And the leering jack-o'-lantern thing was standing on the lip of the pit, looking down at him, eyes afire. It kind of cackled and moaned, and the smile grew wider. Then it leaped into the grave, and Otis just had time to wonder dimly if they had leather jackets where he was going.

The Gift

Monica Hughes

Cindy is totally special. I'm not just saying that because she's my kid sister. She's amazingly pretty, with dark blue eyes and black hair. Mom says that comes from our Irish background and maybe a touch of Spanish blood from when the Armada got wrecked back in 1588. Whatever.

She's also bright, with a great sense of humor. When Mom brought her home from the hospital, I was six years old. I remember holding the tiny bundle in my arms, terrified of dropping her and not very happy at no longer being *numero uno* in the Williams family. Then she opened her eyes and looked up at me. Talk about bonding! I was hooked for life.

So now it's close to her eighth birthday, and I'm hunting for that special gift, something that will clearly say, *Yes, this is for Cindy.* I've saved almost all my baby-sitting money and worn my legs off to the ankles trudging through stores. Nothing's right. Nope, not this . . . Not that either . . .

Then I see the doll. It's in a secondhand store where I've bought some funky clothes and earrings, and at this minute

I'm certainly not looking for Cindy's birthday present. But there she is. Propped up on top of a bookcase full of recycled Harlequin Romances, slumped over to one side, her legs dangling limply over the top shelf, her clothes dirty and torn, her china face filthy.

Little Orphan Annie, I think. But maybe . . . She is not a doll to play with, I realize, but that's okay. Cindy doesn't play with dolls. She collects them. They sit in a row on a shelf in her bedroom. A Spanish dancer, a Dutch doll, baby dolls, and grown-up costumed dolls.

Mentally I wash the dirty face, renew the stuffing in the limp body, and make an exquisite Victorian dress, all lace and tucks, complete with petticoat and frilly underpants. Resurrected in my mind, the doll already seems less abandoned.

I wander around the store, picking up a pair of earrings, holding a T-shirt to my front. I drift over to the bookcase and let my eyes wander up the shelves, pulling out a book, leafing through it, and putting it back. Then I pretend to notice the doll. I look at it, shake my head, look at it again. I'm aware that the owner is watching my performance and cut to the chase.

"I need a birthday present for my kid sister," I say casually. "Nothing expensive. What are you asking for that old doll?"

"Not *old*," she tells me. "Antique." She names a price, and my jaw drops. Now I'm not acting.

"Cindy's not interested in *antiques*," I stammer.

"Then you'd better buy her a Barbie." She turns away with a sneer.

"She's not into Barbies. She likes collecting dolls."

"Well, this one *is* a collectible."

"Terrible condition, though," I bounce back.

"Restoring is part of the collector's challenge." She stands beside me, looking up at the doll.

The bargaining goes on for a while. In the end, I walk out of the store a whole lot poorer, carefully carrying the doll in a cocoon of tissue paper in an old shoebox.

For the next couple of weeks, I work on it in my spare time, which isn't a lot, since I baby-sit Cindy most of the day while Mom sleeps. I wash the doll carefully, patting it dry as if it were a real child. I shampoo and set the hair, and mend the torn places in the body, carefully tucking in new stuffing.

Fiddliest of all are the clothes. As she sat limply in the sec-ondhand store, I had imaginatively clothed the doll in Victorian costume. Imagination is a darn sight easier and quicker than reality, I realize as I struggle with the dinky little seams, make the rows of tucking, and apply the bits of lace I've rescued from Mom's box of leftovers.

Her hair hasn't responded too well to the shampoo, and I can't tame the frizzies, so I make a flowery hat to quench them. With a pearl-headed pin left over from a corsage to hold the hat in place, she looks fantastic. Practically a living, breathing Victorian young lady.

Cindy's face, when she unfolds the tissue wrapping and sees my creation for the first time, makes the trouble and dollars spent totally worthwhile.

"Oh!" she says. She takes a deep breath. "Oh, Trish! Is it really mine?"

"Absolutely. All yours. Happy birthday!" We hug.

She lifts the doll from its nest of paper and hugs it too. Then she exclaims, "Ouch!" and puts a hand to her cheek. She takes her hand away, and I can see a red scratch.

"Cindy, I'm so sorry. That darn hatpin."

"It's okay," Cindy says bravely, but her lip trembles. Mom hurries to bathe her face with a cool, wet cloth, and I find a bead to push over the pointy end of the pin. Cindy is all smiles again.

"What are you going to call her?" Mom asks.

"Her name is Sophie," Cindy says formally, as if the doll has already been named.

"Pretty. What made you think of that?"

Cindy stares. "It's her *name*."

I look at the doll cradled in Cindy's arms, and I see a smear of blood on one cheek. It makes her look raffish, like a child wearing her mother's blush. I take the damp cloth and wipe the stain off the smooth china cheek. The dark blue eyes look blankly into mine. With a jolt, I realize that Sophie looks very like Cindy. The same impossibly dark blue eyes, the same black wavy hair . . .

We all troop upstairs to install Sophie in pride of place in the very middle of the doll shelf. Mom remembers a useless little lace cushion she bought at a church bazaar, and upon this Sophie sits, her back propped against the wall, her skirts spread decorously around her, her feet dangling over the edge of the cushion, her hands neatly folded in her lap.

"There. She looks just like a queen." Cindy backs away, her face beaming. Then we go downstairs to get ready for the party: six of her friends invited for a trip to the water park and cake and ice cream at the mall.

By the time her six frenetic friends have been delivered safely back to their parents, Mom has to get ready for work – night shift at the local hospital – and I shoo Cindy into her bath and bed and collapse myself. Small kids are really tiring, especially when they've OD'd on waterslides and cake.

The moon is shining full on my face when I wake up. I didn't close the curtains properly, and a bar of white light blazes across my bed. I blink and wonder lazily if I have the energy to get up and close the gap. Then I hear the voice. An agitated mutter, going on and on.

"Cindy?" I stumble across my room and into Cindy's. Enough moonlight sifts across the passage that I can see her sitting up in bed, clutching the sheet and staring across the room. I look around, but there's nothing there but the shelf of dolls.

"Don't make me!" she cries out. "I don't want to. Leave me alone."

"Hush, sprout. Nobody can make you do anything you don't want."

"*She* can."

"A bad dream," I tell her firmly. I smooth her sweaty forehead and turn her pillow cool side up and make her lie down again. Her cheek feels hot. Is that the cheek that the pin scratched? Could it be infected? I tell myself not to be stupid, that it was only a pin, after all. I sit on the edge of her bed, stroking her forehead until I hear her breathing evenly, deeply. Then I stumble, yawning, back to bed.

"I had a funny dream," Cindy says over Sunday breakfast.

"What about?" I ask.

She shrugs. "I don't remember. A horrid voice going on and on."

"If it happens again, tell it to go away. Tell it you don't have to listen."

"Okay. Can I have another pancake?"

"Another pancake what?" Mom says.

"With maple syrup." Cindy chuckles. It's a family joke she never tires of. "Maple syrup, *please*," she adds.

While Mom sleeps, I take Cindy to the park to fly her favorite kite. We eat lunch at McDonald's, and later, when Mom is awake, she plays Snakes and Ladders with Cindy while I make macaroni and cheese for supper — my top favorite food. Luckily, Cindy likes it too. Mom doesn't complain and has an extra helping of salad.

"Go away! Go away! I don't have to listen." Cindy's voice penetrates my dreams. Good for her, I think sleepily. Just before I drift off again I hear a sound like a soft crash — can a crash be soft? — then I'm out of it till morning.

Since Dad died, Mom has had to go back to nursing full time. During the holidays, she's usually in bed by the time I get up. It's almost nine o'clock when I wake up to shower and then make fresh orange juice and put out the breakfast cereal. I go upstairs again to wake up Cindy.

"Whoa! What happened in here!" I stop on the threshold. Every one of Cindy's precious dolls, except for Sophie, is lying on the floor. "What did you do that for?"

Cindy sits up in bed and stares. "I didn't do nothing." She shakes her head emphatically.

"Didn't do *anything*," I say automatically. I can see she's telling the truth. The dolls don't even look as if they've been pulled off the shelf. The way they've landed, I'd swear they've been *pushed*. From behind.

Which is crazy. And impossible.

"Breakfast's ready," I tell her. I pick up the dolls one by one and replace them on the shelf. The Spanish dancer has lost her comb and the Japanese geisha her fan. I put them aside.

I must try to glue them back later, I tell myself. I find I'm avoiding Sophie's blank blue stare as I arrange the dolls on either side of her.

"No bad dreams, I hope," I say lightly.

"Nope. I did what you said. I told her I didn't have to listen. Boy, was she *mad!*"

Kids are weird, I think as I go downstairs again to reheat the coffee Mom left after her breakfast.

It's a gorgeous day, and as I eat my toast and drink my coffee I think of possible ways for Cindy and me to spend it.

"The zoo. What about the zoo?"

"Uh-uh."

"You wanna fly kites again?"

She shakes her head.

Even a great relationship has its down moments. I can feel myself getting irritated. What I would really like to do is hang out with my friends, but they don't appreciate being saddled with an eight-year-old, even one as normally sweet-tempered as Cindy.

"What *do* you want to do?" I try to iron the snarl out of my voice.

"Nothing."

"What d'you mean, 'nothing'? You can't do nothing."

"I don't want to go places. I just want to play in my room."

"But it's a gorgeous day. Who knows — tomorrow may be raining."

She shakes her head and sticks out her lower lip. I remember a lesson Mom taught me: compromise. "Okay. I'll give the living room and kitchen a quick vacuuming and make something cold for supper. *Then* we'll go out."

She pushes aside her cereal bowl and runs from the room. I whirl around the downstairs with the vacuum. I make ham sandwiches for lunch, and boil eggs and potatoes for salad for supper. By then, it's almost noon.

"Time to go." I stop outside the door of Cindy's room. She's sitting on the floor with Sophie in her lap.

"All right," she says. But she doesn't move, and I realize that she's talking to the doll. "I promise I'll play with you whenever you want." She waits as if she's listening to a reply. Then she nods. "Of course you come first, silly."

"Time to put Sophie back on the shelf, sprout. We'll go to the park. I've made sandwiches. Come on. The day's wasting."

"Don't want to." Her voice sounds different. Sort of affected.

"Cindy, what's got into you?"

She turns her back, ignoring me, whispering to the doll.

Something snaps in me, and I tear Sophie out of her hands, squeezing her stuffed arms angrily. I dump her on her cushion on the shelf. "There. Stay there," I mutter.

Then I turn round quickly because Cindy is crying – not temper-tantrum tears but real ones, welling out of her eyes and down her cheeks. "You hurt me, Trish," she wails.

"But I didn't even touch you. Hush now, or you'll wake Mom."

She silently holds out her arms, and I can see, clearly marked, red fingermarks, just as if I'd grabbed her hard and pulled her.

"But I didn't . . ." I stop and start again. "The park. Come on, sprout. Get moving."

She sits on the floor and shakes her head stubbornly.

"Cindy, we had a bargain. You got to play. Now it's time for fresh air and exercise."

"I can't."

"What do you mean you can't?"

"She won't let me."

I don't have to ask who *she* is. This is getting out of hand. "She's a doll, Cindy. She can't tell you what to do."

I force her to her feet, down the stairs, out of the house. She starts screaming as soon as we're outdoors. Mrs. Donnelly from next door comes out onto her porch and glares at me as if I'm beating up my kid sister. I get as far as the corner before I give up. Compromise, I remind myself between clenched teeth.

"Look, we'll take Sophie with us to the park. In your wagon, okay?"

The tears stop. It is as if Cindy is listening. But not to me. Then she nods. "Okay."

We set off again. I'm carrying the kite and the backpack with our lunch. Cindy pulls the wagon with Sophie sitting in it, her legs stiffly out in front of her. I feel uneasily that *she* doesn't approve of my compromise. Stupid, I tell myself. She's only a doll, for Pete's sake!

I find us a shady spot under a cottonwood and get the kite started before giving the string to Cindy. It's a perfect day. The kite soars and swoops. It climbs higher and higher, and I can tell Cindy's really enjoying herself. Forgetting.

I relax. Then she stumbles and falls flat, both her hands going out in front of her, the kite sailing up and away, trailing its string.

I run to pick her up. She's not hurt, and I can't imagine what she stumbled over. The grass is totally smooth. "Bad luck about your kite," I say. "Maybe we can find another one like it." I know it's her favorite — a green pterodactyl. She doesn't seem to care, but instead trots back to the tree and picks up Sophie. "I'm sorry," I hear her say. "I do love you best of all. Truly I do."

We eat lunch, and for the rest of the afternoon Cindy plays with Sophie. It's like listening to one half of a telephone conversation filled with meaningful pauses. I find myself checking to see if Sophie's lips are moving as Cindy listens, nods, and talks back. Kids, I tell myself. What imagination! But I feel uneasy, sort of prickly, on edge.

It gets hotter and great castles of cumulus are beginning to pile up around the horizon. Maybe that's what's making me feel jumpy – just the weather. We pack up and walk home. Cindy's so tired she rides in the wagon with Sophie in her lap, and I haul them both. "Nap time, sprout," I say once we're in the house. This time I get no argument.

Later, I peek into her room and see them both laid out on the bed. Cindy's sound asleep, a faint dew of perspiration on her forehead. Beside her, Sophie's eyes are also closed. As I tiptoe out, something makes me turn at the door. My heart jolts, and I find I'm clutching the door frame for support.

Sophie's eyes are open, and she seems to be staring balefully at me. How can glass eyes be so hate-filled? How can they be *open*? She's lying flat on her back. Everyone knows how sleeping-doll eyes work.

I run downstairs and turn on the TV. When Mom wakes up, I'm staring at the screen, watching some dumb soap. I tell her I've made potato salad for supper.

"Great. I don't know how I'd manage without you, Trish." She hesitates. "Is it too much for you? Baby-sitting Cindy all summer? I could probably afford to hire a housekeeper, just for a month or so."

I stare. "What brought that on, Mom? I'm fine." I wonder what a housekeeper would make of Sophie.

"It's just . . ." She stops again. "You wouldn't ever *hurt* Cindy, would you? It's just that I saw these great bruises on her arms, as if someone had grabbed hold of her . . ."

Bruises? Then I remember the red marks on her arms after I snatched Sophie away. What can I say? That I roughed up her doll and the marks magically transferred? No way! But what else can I say? I let myself get mad that Mom would even think that I'd hurt my sister. "Boy, you've got a suspicious mind! That's really insulting. If you want to know, she tripped in the park when she was flying her kite – lost the kite too, though she didn't seem to mind."

So Mom apologizes, and that's it. But it makes me think, more than I've allowed myself to think up till now. The bruises magically transferred? How could that possibly be? But what other explanation is there?

At suppertime, Cindy's still asleep and I have to wake her. Then Mom hurries off to the hospital. The thunder clouds are really piling up now, and the sky has a dirty, yellow-gray look. It's stiflingly hot in spite of open doors and windows and the fan going.

Cindy plays in her room and I let her. What else can I do? But I insist on regular bedtime. She doesn't seem to mind, as long as Sophie gets to lie beside her.

I'm still up when the voices start. *Voices?* Nonsense. There's only Cindy up there. I run upstairs, accompanied by a flash of light and a following roll of thunder.

"You have to play as long as I want you to." Pause. "No, you're not tired. Wake up, I tell you. Wake up!"

I turn on the light. Cindy is sitting up in bed, Sophie in her lap. Her cheeks are flushed and wet, her hair tangled, and her eyes are full of despair. "Trish, I'm so sleepy, and she won't leave me alone."

"Give her to me," I manage to say and gently – oh, so gently – I lift Sophie from her lap and replace her on her cushion on the shelf.

"Lie down, sprout."

"Don't go," she whispers, looking past me at the doll shelf.

"I won't."

"Trish, I've got a secret."

"What is it?"

She leans against me as I sit beside her on the bed and whispers breathily in my ear, "I'm sorry, Trish, but I hate her."

I whisper back, "Me too." Then I snuggle down beside her. "Go to sleep, Cindy. We'll deal with it in the morning."

She's asleep in a minute, and I lie beside her, staring at the ceiling. Now and then a flash of lightning illuminates the room and the thunder rolls by. How can I deal with this? I think. I need help. But who can I tell? What can I say? They won't believe me. Even Mom will think I'm crazy.

I must have fallen asleep, because a sudden crash of thunder jolts me awake and I realize that Cindy is no longer beside me. I sit up and stare. The lightning illuminates the room. She's on the floor, with Sophie in her lap. And now I can hear *two* voices. She must be getting stronger, I think, and a shiver runs down my spine.

"You're my friend. You've got to play with me. Now smarten up and play properly."

"I can't. Sophie, I'm so tired. I wanna go to bed."

"No, you don't. I'm in charge, you know. I tell *you* what to do."

The voice is sharp and penetrating. I can feel it like a splinter under my skin. Without thinking, I jump off the bed and snatch the doll from Cindy's arms. I shake her and shake her. "Stop this right now. Leave her alone," I scream.

I can let the stuffing out of you, I think wildly. I can throw you in the garbage. Break your stupid china face.

Then, as I look past the blank face, the hard blue eyes, I see Cindy. She's still sitting on the floor, but she is being shaken by some invisible force, shaken so hard that her head bobs back and forth. "Don't," she gasps as the breath is jolted out of her body. "You're hurting me, Trish."

Somehow I control myself, put Sophie back on the shelf, and gather Cindy up in my arms. "I'm sorry, love. I didn't think . . ."

"Don't you love me anymore?" she wails.

I wind my arms around her and hold her tight. I can't answer. I sit on the floor, rock her to and fro, and stare past her at the doll on the shelf. Every time the lightning shimmers across the room, the glass eyes gleam.

I can't let the stuffing out of you, I think. I can't break you or put you in the garbage, or even give you away.

What *can* I do?

The thunder rolls away and the house is so quiet that I can hear the water dripping off the leaves outside. Slowly the night passes and the sky lightens. I hear the dawn chorus of birds begin as they sleepily awake to the new day. I hold my little sister close in my arms and grieve.

What have I done?

The Gun Show

Ed Gorman

Indian summer. Saturday afternoon. Perfect smoky autumn.
The gun show was being held on an old fairgrounds, in a big exhibition hall, a building badly in need of white paint, a new roof, and new plumbing. The urinal was so old it was a long, white, rust-stained latrine.

The license plates of a dozen states could be found on the cars that packed the parking lot. The fashion for the day ran largely to camouflage and khaki. There were a lot of fathers and sons, but a good number of women, too. The smell of fresh popcorn, grilling hot dogs, and beer in the various concession stands lent the festivities the aroma of a carnival midway. Everything echoed in the huge hall. There was an unrelenting din of voices, weapons being locked and loaded, arguments, jokes, and a variety of radios playing country songs.

Todd Andrews stood in the entrance of the vast building. Gun collectors of every kind had set up booths, selling everything from weapons of the Revolutionary War to today's most efficient killing machines.

Todd was seventeen. He'd driven downstate from Oak
Park in his parents' car. Ninety miles. A year ago, after his
younger brother, Michael, had killed three of his ninth-grade
classmates, Todd had done a little investigating and come up
with his theory. This was when his folks sent him to a psy-
chiatrist named Dr. Spangler, a cold and patronizing man
who couldn't stop himself from smirking whenever Todd
brought up the subject of the gun dealer.

Todd didn't have any choice. His parents didn't believe
him; Dr. Spangler didn't believe him; and the one and only
time he'd raised the subject with the police officers who
investigated Michael, they only stared at him with pity.

Todd went to the booth.

The man's name was Linc Reynolds. He was tall, slim,
angular. He wore a faded Levi's shirt with the arms cut off and
tight faded jeans with a belt made of Navajo turquoise. He
had a gaunt face and deep-set blue eyes shadowed beneath
the brim of a black, flat-brimmed western hat. You could find
a dozen of his kind at any truck stop between here and
Bakersfield or here and the Gulf of Mexico. Except for the
eyes. The combination of amusement and anger was something Todd had never seen before. And it scared him.

Reynolds recognized him immediately. "You're persistent,
kid, I got to give you that."

"I want the gun."

Reynolds smiled. It was a slow, expansive smile, like a drawl.
"I got a lot of guns here, kid. Which one you fixin' to buy?"

"You know the one I mean."

"You see it anywhere in the booth here?"

Todd said, "The one you gave my brother. The one you
gave those other kids at the other schools."

Reynolds tamped a Marlboro from his pack, lit it with a
stick match he ignited with a thumbnail, and inhaled deeply.

"I don't reckon I know what you're talking about, pardner."

Two boys about Todd's age came up. One was chunky, with long, dirty hair and a camouflage vest. The other was skinny. He had horn-rimmed glasses, a butch haircut, and a button-down shirt. He looked intelligent.

Todd instantly sensed Reynolds's interest in the skinny boy.

"Well, now, pardner, how can I help you?" Reynolds said to the boy.

Reynolds had a type he went after. Todd had laid out on the bed all seven newspaper photos of the shooters. They'd all looked sort of bookish, like this kid.

"Get away from here," Todd said to the boy. "I know what I'm talking about. He's going to give you a special gun. And believe me, you don't want it."

The chunky kid looked at Todd and grinned. "Some kinda magic gun, is it?"

Reynolds came around the side of his booth and grabbed Todd by the back of the shirt and the seat of his pants.

Everybody around the booth started watching as Reynolds scooted Todd down the long concrete aisle to the front door of the place, where an off-duty policeman watched over everything as he drank a can of Diet Pepsi.

"This one's been givin' me trouble, Merle, and I wanted his butt kicked off this fairgrounds right here and right now."

Merle set his can down. He had big Vs of sweat under the arms of his light blue shirt.

"He's evil!" Todd shouted. "He isn't who he seems to be! I know who he really is!"

People were smiling. Wasn't often you got to see a crazy kid making a fool of himself like this. It was embarrassing, was what it was. But still kinda fun to see. Like one of them "reality" cop shows on the tube.

On the way to the front gate, Merle said, "You on some kinda drugs?"

"No, sir."

"You drinkin' somethin'?"

"Just pop."

"How come you got all het up, then?"

Todd was going to tell him the whole thing, but then he decided against it. He felt tired suddenly. He just didn't want to have to go through the whole thing only to see Merle smirk a little and shake his head in pity, the way most folks did when Todd told them.

At the front gate, Merle said, "You come back through this gate, you're gonna get arrested. You understand that?"

"Yes, sir."

"You just clear out, you hear me?"

"Yes, sir."

Merle gave him a hard and very official police stare, and then he turned around and walked back to the exhibition hall.

The skinny kid and his friend didn't come out for another hour and a half.

Todd had moved his car so he had a clear view of the front gate. He watched the two high-school boys jump into a new, white VW Bug and pull away.

He followed them.

The town, New Rock, looked to be prosperous and modern. The Hello sign said 31,000 was the population. A lot of the homes were laid out in housing developments and looked recent. This had to be some kind of bedroom community for commuters.

The skinny kid, the driver, let the chunky kid off in front of a split-level ranch house. A bald man in khaki shorts and a University of Illinois T-shirt was mowing the lawn. Skinny kid and chunky kid talked a few minutes, the latter leaning back into the VW so he could hear above the mower, and then the car took off again.

Todd knew he had to do it now.

Finding the right spot was all he had to do.

The VW wound through a deep forest and then came out along a sun-sparkling river. At a convenience store, the VW whipped in and parked. Todd wondered if the kid had suddenly figured out that he was being followed.

The store had one of those sickeningly cute names – Kash 'n Kwik – and looked to be pretty much empty at this lazy point in the afternoon.

Todd went over and leaned against the VW.

When the kid came out, he stopped and said, "You're the kid from the gun show."

"Yeah."

The boy looked nervous. "I don't want any hassles."

"I just want to talk to you, is all. What's your name?"

"Why?"

Todd put his hand out. "Mine's Todd."

The kid glanced anxiously back at the store, obviously hoping somebody was watching. Then he took Todd's hand. "Randy."

"You take the gun?"

"Yeah. Why?"

"He didn't charge you for it, did he?"

"No. He said it just wasn't much good to him. Just an old .45 from the Korean War, is all."

Todd thought a second. "You see that river over there?"

"Yeah. Sure."

"You should take that .45 and throw it in there."

Randy grinned. "Boy, that'd be pretty stupid."

"Or you should sell it to me. I'll give you a hundred dollars."

Randy had to be thinking about the swift profit he'd be making. But then he shook his head. "I guess not."

"Why not?"

Randy shrugged. "I guess I just like the gun, is all. There's something about it."

"Oh, yeah, there's something about it, all right."

Then he told Randy what he knew about the gun. How his brother had killed three of his friends and then himself. And how Todd had traced the gun to the traveling gun dealer named Linc. And how Todd had then done some research at the library and found out that in every town where Linc and the gun show had appeared, a teenager – usually a boy, but twice girls – had shortly after used a .45 to kill himself, fellow students, or innocent bystanders in robberies.

"It wasn't them that did the killing," Todd said. "It was the gun. There's something about it. Somehow, it always ends up in Linc's hands again, and he gives it free to a teenager. Now you've got it."

"My dad always says that guns don't kill people – people kill people. He's in the NRA."

"None of that matters," Todd said. "All I'm talking about is this particular gun. I've seen what happens, believe me. I lost my brother because of that gun. Now, the best thing you can do is throw it in that river over there or give it to me."

Randy was silent a moment and then bolted for the driver's side of his car. "I gotta be home for supper. And I'd appreciate it if you wouldn't lean against my car. It's new."

Then the small import was whining backwards in reverse, and Randy was wheeling quickly away from the store.

This time, Todd stayed a full block behind him. He had to find out where Randy lived.

It was two hours later when Randy left his house, climbed into his VW, and sped off. But not before he shoved something into the glove compartment. Todd knew what it was, too.

Todd took a deep breath and steadied himself. This was going to be the most difficult part of it all. He could well end up in jail.

He pressed the doorbell, waited.

A slender, pretty woman in a white blouse and jeans came to the door. "Yes?"

"Are you Randy's mother?"

"Yes. He just left about two minutes ago."

"I know. I watched him."

Her face showed suspicion. "Is there something I can help you with?"

"I'd like to speak to you and your husband."

Instead of answering, she turned around and said, "Bill? Bill, would you come here a minute, please?"

Bill, Mr. Bennett, was a perfect mate for his wife. A pleasant-looking person of middle-age, balding, slightly nervous blue eyes, jeans and button-down white shirt worn loose.

She said, "He says he wants to talk to us." She indicated the boy in the door. She sounded both nervous and angry. He had disrupted her smooth-running life, this young stranger.

"About what?"

"He didn't say."

"It's important," Todd said.

"And it's about what exactly?"

"Randy," Todd said. "And the gun he got today."

Mr. Bennett smiled. "That old .45? Why, that's nothing. I'm not even sure it'll shoot."

"Oh, it'll shoot, all right." Todd looked directly at him. "It's killed several people in the past year."

"Oh? And how do you know that?" Mr. Bennett said.

"Because my brother used it, for one thing. And after he killed his friends, he killed himself with it."

"Maybe we'd better call the police," Mrs. Bennett said. "He's making me very nervous."

Mr. Bennett shook his head. "Let's let him in and talk first, Lisa. At least see what he's got to say."

"I'd rather call the police," she said.

But two minutes later, Todd was seating himself on the couch. "Let me tell you about the gun first. Then you can call the police – if you still want to."

Randy Bennett could feel the tension as soon as Mr. Patterson let him in the front door. Cindy Patterson had been Randy's girlfriend for a year, and a rough year it had been. Randy was a possessive boy who got jealous over just about anything Cindy did that she didn't have his approval for.

Going to the mall with girlfriends. Going to the Cineplex with her older sister. Swimming at the public pool. Doing her homework at the library. Randy saw all these as opportunities for Cindy to meet boys and flirt with them. Sometimes, he got so worked up he couldn't sleep or eat. He'd never hurt her in any way, wouldn't, hated boys who hurt girls. But his jealousy got so bad . . .

He was sort of on probation with her folks. They didn't want Cindy to go out with him anymore. She was young.

She should be enjoying her life. And they were afraid of what Randy – who could be a nice kid but had a bad temper – might do to their daughter some night. Stuff like that was on TV all the time.

The relationship with her parents had deteriorated to the point where Mrs. Patterson wouldn't even come in and say hello. She always stayed upstairs so she wouldn't have to speak to him.

Mr. Patterson didn't say anything. Just let Randy sit there. Mr. Patterson was watching a Cubs game. Randy had no interest in baseball.

Cindy came downstairs in a white blouse and jeans. So pretty. And such a body. God. He was so lucky. He had to be careful. He didn't want to blow up again, because he knew that would be the end. Even if Cindy wanted to see him, her parents wouldn't let her.

"Night, Daddy," she said, and gave him a kiss on the cheek.

"Midnight, remember," said Mr. Patterson.

"No problem, Mr. Patterson," Randy said, trying to sound friendly.

He was just holding the front door for Cindy to walk outside when he saw the red convertible. Mike Nolan. The basketball star who'd been sniffing around Cindy ever since Randy had started dating her.

On the drive to the Cineplex, Cindy seemed cordial, sweet. But Randy couldn't stop thinking of Mike Nolan. Had his cruising past Cindy's house been a coincidence, or was there something going on here that Randy didn't know about? Maybe Cindy was sneaking out on him.

"You all right?" Cindy said.

"Yeah, fine," he said, smiling over at her.

But when he looked at her closely, he wondered if those were lies he saw in her eyes.

Maybe there really *was* something going on between her and Nolan. . . .

"I mean this in the nicest possible way," Randy's mother said after Todd finished telling her his story. "I'd like you to give me the phone number of your parents, and I'd like to call them, and I'd like them to come and pick you up."

"You seem like a very nice boy," Randy's father said. "But maybe you need to . . . you know, talk to someone."

Todd smiled sadly. "A shrink? I've seen three of them."

"What you're talking about . . ." Mrs. Bennett said gently. "Well, it's just not possible, Todd."

"Are you hungry?" Mr. Bennett asked. He spoke with great by-God enthusiasm, as if a burger and fries might be able to cure this lad's madness.

Mrs. Bennett came over, sat next to Todd on the couch, and put her arm around him. "Why don't you give me your folks' phone number, hon? You can sit here and talk to Bill."

Todd's head dropped and his hands covered his face.

He hadn't expected them to believe him, and they hadn't let him down. They were already picking out psychiatric hospitals for him.

Finally, he couldn't stand it anymore. They were about halfway to the Cineplex when Randy said, "You see Mike today?"

"Who?"

"Don't give me any of your lies. You know who. Mike Nolan."

"Why would I see Mike Nolan?"

"Gosh, let me think," he said. "Maybe because you've been sneaking around with him behind my back!"

"Randy! That's crazy!"

"Oh, yeah. I suppose you didn't see him drive by your house back there."

"No, as I matter of fact, I didn't. And anyway, I can't stand him. He's so conceited."

This time when he looked at her, he was miserable. "Just tell me the truth, that's all I ask. Just tell me the truth."

He sounded – much as he didn't want to – as if he was going to cry.

Todd saw that he was going to have to humor them. He gave Mrs. Bennett his home phone number. She went in and called. No answer. They'd be at the club tonight. Every Saturday night. In the sixties, his father had been something of a hippie, but then he got heavily into greed. He belonged to the most important of three country clubs in their small city, and he never missed a Saturday night dance there.

"Well, why don't I fix you something to eat?" Randy's mother said when she came back. "I can try your folks again in a little while. How does a ham sandwich sound?"

"I guess I am kind of hungry."

Mrs. Bennett seemed to equate hunger with sanity the same way her husband did. She got this huge grin on her face and went off to make him some dinner.

They watched a Harrison Ford movie on HBO. Todd ate his sandwich and potato chips and drank his Pepsi. A couple of hours went by. And then the phone rang.

Mrs. Bennett went to pick it up in the kitchen.

Mr. Bennett didn't seem especially interested in who was calling.

Todd listened intently.

Randy's mother screamed, "Oh, God, no! Oh, God, no!"

There really wasn't anything to do at the hospital. Technically, Randy had died while he was in the ambulance. The doctor gave Mrs. Bennett a couple of Valiums. She needed them badly. Mr. Bennett had become one of the living dead. Sorrow and silence.

As the three made their way out to Mr. Bennett's car, a uniformed cop came up and gave Randy's father a hug.

"Ted's his brother," Mrs. Bennett said.

Mr. Bennett started crying. Ted just held him. Ted was crying too.

When they were both filling their handkerchiefs, Ted said, "I found out what I could. The gal – Cindy, right? – she said they were having this argument, he was accusing her of sneaking off with somebody else or something like that. She opened the glove compartment to get some Kleenex because she was crying and all, and she saw this gun and picked it up. And she said she held it for a minute and then – and she admits he wasn't hurting her in any way or even threatening to – she just started pulling the trigger. Six shots in the head and chest. Her parents said they couldn't believe it. They were always afraid Randy would hurt *her*. I guess the girl said it was like she didn't have any control. The gun was just firing itself."

Todd kept looking to see if any of this was upsetting Randy's mother. But she looked too stoned on the Valium to get excited about anything. Thank God.

Todd slept in his own bed that night.

His parents, of course, wanted to know where he had been till three in the morning – *God, we were so worried, Todd. Please don't ever stay out that late again without calling us, all right?* – and what he had been doing.

He told a believable lie. Told them there'd been a kegger. Said he had had just a couple small paper cups and had been fine to drive.

He felt sorry for Mr. and Mrs. Bennett. And for Cindy's parents.

On Monday he went back to school, and after a couple of days the worst of the weekend started to fade. There was a girl he was interested in. And a graduation car his folks were going to buy for him – his choice. And he decided there wasn't anything he could do about the gun show and Linc at all.

On Friday night, just as he was going out, his mother knocked on his bedroom door and said, "Phone call for you, hon."

He picked it up. "Hello?"

"It's Bill Bennett, Todd. Randy's dad."

"How're things going, Mr. Bennett?" he said. He knew it was an inane question, but he didn't know what else to say.

"Lisa barely made it through the funeral."

"I'm sorry."

"He's got her drugged up all the time now. I guess it's the only way she can handle it for the time being." He paused. "I believe you now, Todd. About Linc. Cindy would never do anything like that. Not ever."

"Well, you may believe me, Mr. Bennett. But nobody else does."

"We're going to get him, Todd. You and me. I bought this gun-show guide. He's in Iowa next weekend. Near Cedar Rapids. That's not far for either of us. I'll be there. How about you?"

Todd hesitated. Then: "Yeah, I'll be there, Mr. Bennett."

"I'll meet you at noon at the front gate."

"Noon," Todd said. "Noon."

"God, I hope there's some way we can stop him."

"I hope so too, Mr. Bennett."

Then he went over and picked up the framed photograph of his brother.

Noon. Noon, indeed.

Personality Problem

Joe R. Lansdale

Yeah, I know, Doc, I look terrible and don't smell any better. But you would, too, if you stayed on the go like I do, had a peg sticking out of either side of your neck and this crazy scar across your forehead. You'd think they could have told me to use cocoa butter on the place after they took the stitches out, but naw, no way. They didn't care if I had a face like a train track. No meat off *their* noses.

And how about this get-up? Nice, huh? Early wino or late drug addict? You ought to walk down the street wearing this mess – you really get the stares. Coat's too small, pants too short. And these boots, now, they get the blue ribbon. You know, I'm only six-five, but with these on I'm nearly seven feet! That's some heels.

But listen, how can I do any better? I can't even afford to buy myself a tie at the Goodwill, let alone get myself a new suit of clothes. And have you ever tried to fit someone my size? This shoulder is higher than the other one. The arms don't quite match, and . . . well, you see the problem. I tell you, Doc, it's no bed of roses.

Worst part of it is how people are always running from me, and throwing things, and trying to set me on fire. Oh, that's the classic one. I mean, I've been frozen for a while, covered in mud, you name it, but the old favorite is the torch. And I *hate* fire. Which reminds me, think you could refrain from smoking, Doc? Sort of makes me nervous.

See, I was saying about the fire. They've trapped me in windmills, castles, labs. All sorts of places. Some guy out there in the crowd always gets the wise idea about the fire, and there we go again, Barbecue City. Let me tell you, Doc, I've been lucky. Spell that l-u-c-k-y. We're talking big lucky here. I mean, that's one reason I look as bad as I do. These holes in this already ragged suit . . . Yeah, that's right, bend over. Right there, see? This patch of hide was burned right off my head, Doc, and it didn't feel like no sunburn either. I mean, it hurt.

And I had no childhood. Just a big, dumb boy all my life. No dates. No friends. Nothing. Just this personality complex, and this feeling that everybody hates me on sight.

If I ever get my hands on Victor or Igor, oh, boy . . . Gonna have to snap 'em, Doc. And I can do it, believe me. That's where they crapped in the mess kit, Doc. They made me strong, real strong.

Give me a dime. Yeah, thanks.

Now watch this. Between thumb and finger. *Uhhhh.* How about that? Flat as a pancake.

Yeah, you're right. I'm getting a little excited. I'll lie back and take it easy.

Say, do you smell smoke?

Doc?

Doc?

Doc, damn you, put out that fire! Not you, too! Hey, I'm not a bad guy, really. Come back here, Doc! Don't leave me in here. Don't lock that door!

The Flat-Brimmed Hat

Nancy Etchemendy

Balanced on the crumbly bedrock cliff at the edge of the old V & T grade, Kathy wondered whether she really wanted to do it, and if so, whether this was really the *way* she wanted to do it. She took a deep breath, then another and another. The jagged rocks and the green valley far below flickered like an old-time movie. Feeling dizzy, she backed up a step and forced herself to breathe more evenly. If she was going to do it, she wanted to do it on purpose, not just hyperventilate herself into unconsciousness and drop over the edge like a sack of potatoes.

The thin, sweet call of a mountain bluebird drifted down to her from a nearby juniper. The wild smells of sagebrush and piñon pine and sun-warmed rocks rode on the back of the wind that came up the grade. She really wanted to do it. There was, after all, more to life than bluebirds and sagebrush. She stepped forward, closed her eyes, ducked her head, and stuck her arms out in front of her. The whole business would be much easier if she pretended she was jumping off the high dive at the municipal swimming pool. One, two, three. She bent her knees, considered holding her nose, then realized she didn't need to. Not this time.

Someone grabbed her by the shoulder. A resonant contralto poured through the high desert stillness. "Hey, cookie. For Chrissakes, give us both a break. You don't really want to do that."

Kathy went rigid, opened her eyes, and silently mouthed the words, "Hell, hell, hell."

Perhaps she had made a mistake. Perhaps she hadn't walked four hours to get to this place. Perhaps this wasn't really the summit of a road so dilapidated that only hikers, horses, and lunatics in Jeeps dared traverse it. No. She was incapable of that particular mistake. She had lived down there in the frigging valley all her life. She knew nobody came to this place. The old-timers had forgotten about it, and the newcomers didn't care about good views unless they could see them from a living-room window.

There were chinks in Kathy's black despair. And anger, like blasting powder, was packed inside them all. She curled her hands into hard rock fists and turned around.

A small woman stood before her, slender hands settled on slender hips. The woman regarded Kathy with sunlit brown eyes and an infuriating half-smile. She wore an embroidered cotton shirt like the ones Kathy had often admired in the window of Parker's Saddle Shop. But the flat-brimmed hat that rode far back on her short, glossy curls looked South American, and the cut of her high-waisted denims marked her as a city jerk. Kathy put on the sneer she used whenever she had to deal with unpleasant people — her drunken stepfather, the landlady's bitchy daughter, and lately Reese Vanderberg as well.

"Who the hell are you? Why don't you just mind your own damn business?" Kathy spit the words out like lit firecrackers.

The woman grinned. She had strong, white teeth. A network of spider's-web laugh-lines appeared at the corners of her eyes. She held out her left hand. A jagged, pale scar ran from the first joint of her index finger to the second.

Kathy knew the scar. She had one exactly like it on her own left index finger. She blinked, struggling to remember whether she had actually jumped off the cliff. Maybe she was dreaming this on the way to the ground. Or maybe she was already dead.

"Just call me Kate," said the woman. "Whether you like it or not, my own damn business includes yours."

"Huh?" said Kathy, scratching her nose. It burned. She'd been out in the sun too long.

"Sweetie, you don't have to understand it, just believe it. I'm you. I'm the woman you're going to be twenty years from now. Look at me. Why are you trying to screw me up like this?"

Kathy squinted. Now that she thought of it, the woman did look a little familiar, in a middle-aged kind of way.

Kate took a cellophane-wrapped cigar out of her pocket. She offered it to Kathy. "No thanks," said Kathy. "They make me sick."

"Yeah, they used to make me sick, too." Chuckling, Kate peeled away the cellophane. "Ten years from now, you'll buy a sports car and take up smoking just because you like the idea of a woman driving fast cars and smoking good cigars."

"Oh, yeah?" said Kathy. She was beginning to feel the way she had years ago after she had drunk a bottle of vanilla with a friend – a little queasy and not altogether certain about the line between what was real and what was not.

Kate stuck the cigar in her mouth and sucked on it, unlit. She took Kathy firmly by the arm and led her away from the precipice, back onto the road.

"So what's bothering you this time? I can't quite remember," she said, her words wet and pleasant.

"If you were really me, you'd remember," said Kathy.

Kate laughed and nipped the end off the cigar with her large, familiar teeth. "Sweetie, you're so dramatic. I admit you don't come this close very often, but you think about it all the time. How the hell am I supposed to keep one trauma separate from the next?"

"I *don't* think about it all the time!" said Kathy.

Kate snorted as she lit a wooden match and cupped it expertly away from the breeze. "Give me a break," she said, puffing until a cloud of white smoke rose from between her hands.

Kathy kicked a pebble. She listened as it rattled down the precipice, striking other rocks on its way to the ground. She shivered. "I got jilted."

"Oh, yeah," said Kate. "I remember now. That golden-haired jerk. Reese What's-his-name."

"Reese Vanderberg is not a jerk. And how would you know? You can't even get his name right."

"Look. I can't get his name right because twenty years from now, *you* won't be able to get his name right. Twenty years from now, Reese Vanderberg will be an insurance salesman with a Lincoln Continental and two preppy jerk kids, whom he will have gotten from that blonde airhead, Sally What's-her-name. Believe me, cookie, there are better things than that in store for you."

Kathy kicked another pebble. "Sally, huh? Yeah. Sally's a creep. And if Reese would rather have Sally, then he's a creep, too."

"Come on. It's not that he'd rather have Sally. And it's not as if you're up here getting ready to jump off a cliff just because Vanderberg jilted you. You say that to me because it's what you'd say to some stranger. But we both know there's more to it than that."

Kathy had sat awake in a chair all night, swept and tumbled by the old, familiar river of dark thoughts. Reese had tried to make love to her, just as all the others had, and she had tried to let him, just as she always did. But her body had betrayed her, in the pattern that had grown smooth through repetition – smooth as a stone in a glacial creek. She had stiffened, pulled back. She had felt the surprise in his hands, saw it flutter like the shadow of a luna moth across his face. She'd grabbed her clothes and run. And Reese had shouted after her, "Bitch! Prick-teasing bitch!" Just like they all did.

She hunched her shoulders and looked over at Kate. Kate wore the dusty hat as if it were a part of her, tipped back in an easy way to reveal damp curls just beginning to turn gray around her ears. Her whole body told a story of pleasure, in the swing of her shoulders as she walked, in the rise and fall of her small breasts as she tasted the sweet tobacco smoke. The lines around Kate's eyes and mouth looked custom-made to mysterious specifications. Those lines cradled smiles, frowns, and dreams the way Kathy had always wanted to cradle a man. She was beautiful.

A dull red flower of grief blossomed inside her. She could never be like that. *Never.* A tear splattered onto her boot. "Hell," said Kathy.

Kate shoved a handkerchief into Kathy's hand. Kathy scrubbed viciously at her eyes. The handkerchief was made of lavender silk and had a violet embroidered on it. It smelled like cigars. She wadded it into a wrinkled ball and flung it back at Kate. "Now I know you're not me," she said. "I wouldn't be caught dead carrying around a thing like that."

Kate stuck the handkerchief back in her pants pocket and gave Kathy a sidelong frown. She turned her gaze back to the rutted road and the junipers that clung to the hillside above it. "All right. You want to know why you're gonna be carrying silk handkerchiefs around someday? Because there's a man in your future who likes them."

Kathy shook her head. "There's no man in my future."

"Suit yourself," said Kate, shrugging.

Kathy wondered why she would want a man in her future anyway. She shoved her hands deep into the pockets of her wash-softened Levi's and found the arrowhead Reese had given her. She rubbed her thumb hard along the sharp flint edge. She thought about the way her father had beaten her mother until she couldn't stand up anymore. She thought about her stepfather, who acted like a stud in rut every time he got drunk. Her heart kept telling her they weren't all like that. But her body just wouldn't believe it.

Kathy looked at Kate again. Kate smiled at her. Kate's face seemed so much at home with smiles. Was it true? Was it possible that Kathy's own face would someday look like that? In the desert sun, something sparkled on one of the fingers of Kate's left hand. A plain gold wedding ring. Kathy blinked, dazzled.

They had been walking as they talked, Kathy following the older woman down the rutted, white road, so preoccupied with her own pain that she paid no attention. Now they rounded a curve, and there, crouched like a steel tiger, sat a Jeep, almost brand new, with all the extras, the kind Kathy had always wanted. A light coating of dust covered its deep burgundy paint. Kathy stared at it, dreaming of places a machine like that could take her, of hillsides and valleys and canyons a million miles away.

"Is that yours? Where'd you get it?"

Kate rubbed her neck slowly, gazing at the Jeep as if she herself found it somewhat mysterious. "Yeah. It's mine. I bought it about six months ago from a guy in Manhattan who told me it could take me places I'd never believe." She gave Kathy a little grin. "I guess he was right."

"Manhattan?" said Kathy.

"Yeah. Manhattan," said Kate, eyes sparkling. "Hop in."

Kathy climbed into the passenger seat, yelping as the heat from the sun-baked black Naugahyde crept through her thin shirt. Kate tossed her hat into the back, ran her fingers through her sweat-soaked hair. She winked.

"What do you think, sweetie? Isn't this better than some blond jerk's Lincoln Continental?"

Kathy grinned. "Could be," she said.

Kate caressed the gearshift lever and twisted the key in the ignition. "Put your seat belt on, cookie."

The Jeep roared and leapt off in a cloud of sand and thunder. Kathy clung to the seat the way she had clung to Reese when he took her on the double Ferris wheel at the county fair.

Kate drove like a maniac, laughing as they fishtailed around curves and sailed airborne over chuckholes and washouts. The cigar jutted from the corner of her mouth, alternately emitting vast wind-blown clouds and waving as Kate chewed on it.

At the top of the V & T grade, Kate shifted down and the Jeep's fat tires screamed as they grabbed the pavement of the main road to Silver City, the half-abandoned mining town on the other side of the hills. They roared like a fire engine past the crumbling graveyard and the entrance to the old Fairman Tunnel. They sprayed dust at the Sutro Hotel and startled the mangy brown dog that lay in the sun on Main Street. When they skidded to a stop in front of Old Pete's Crystal Saloon, Kathy discovered that she was out of breath, and her fingers ached from hanging on so tightly. She wanted more.

"Come on. I'll buy you a drink," said Kate, clapping the flat-brimmed hat onto her head.

Kathy wobbled into the dark coolness of the saloon like a sailor who has just left his ship. Wooden ceiling fans stirred the dry air above her head. A row of slot machines stood against one wall. Shelves lined the other walls, crowded with bits of junk that Old Pete had collected – rocks with fool's gold embedded in them, broken arrowheads, rusty mill gears, and pieces of peeling harness. A jukebox played soft country music from a corner in the back. Kathy climbed onto a stool beside Kate at the massive oak bar.

"Afternoon, ladies. What'll it be?" said Old Pete, wiping his hands on his dirty white apron.

"Double bourbon, neat," said Kate.

"Uh . . . root beer," said Kathy.

Pete washed and dried two glasses. He smiled, revealing a mouth full of night, marred only by two brownish teeth. He contemplated Kate and Kathy with friendly eyes that too many years of sun had made wet and milky. "Mother and daughter, right?" he said.

"Guess again," said Kate.

Pete puckered his thin, dry lips. "Sisters?"

"Yeah, something like that." She winked and picked up their drinks.

Kate led Kathy to a table where they could watch the wind blowing dust along the wooden sidewalks outside. Kathy gazed at her as she took off her hat and tossed it easily onto the seat of the nearest chair. Was it true? Kathy imagined two people standing in a mountain stream. Would water that had touched her ankles touch Kate's someday?

"Who are you . . . really?" she asked softly.

Kate rubbed her thumb across the ridges of the bourbon glass. In the dim light of the saloon, her eyes were black lakes. "I swear to you, this is the truth. This morning I woke up just after sunrise, and I got dressed, and I went for a walk in Central Park. I thought, I'm thirty-seven years old and it's June twenty-first, and twenty years ago to the day, I almost jumped off a cliff. I would have done it. Except a woman named Kate stopped me."

She lifted the bourbon and took a long swallow. "I thought about how fine the morning sun always looks, whether I see it on a wild lake or a row of city windows. And I knew it was time to go back, time to find you. I just knew what to do. Someday you will too."

Kathy sipped at her root beer. It was too sweet and not very cold, but her throat cried out for something to soothe away the sudden dryness. "Central Park? That's in New York, isn't it?"

Kate smiled and nodded. She slipped her wedding ring off and slid it across the table to Kathy. Kathy picked it up. It felt heavy and warm and real. She closed her eyes and pressed the ring hard into her palm, trying to imagine a life that included things like Central Park, and Manhattan, and South American hats, and a man who loved a woman who smoked cigars and carried a lavender silk handkerchief crumpled up in her pocket.

"Trust me, cookie," said Kate. "Your future is worth staying around for."

One tear, then another, dropped onto the shining tabletop between Kathy's hands. She slid the ring back to Kate. "Promise?" she whispered.

"I promise."

Kate finished her bourbon in a long, last swallow, stood up, and grinned. "People are waiting for me," she said. "Good-bye, cookie. Take care of yourself." She turned and walked through the saloon doors to the street.

Several seconds passed before Kathy realized that Kate had forgotten her hat. "Kate!" she shouted. "Wait a minute!"

She shoved her chair back, grabbed the hat, and ran outside. She squinted up and down the sun-bleached street. But the wooden sidewalks and the dilapidated buildings stood deserted in the dry wind. The old dog had not stirred from his place in the middle of the road. The Jeep had disappeared. And Kate was nowhere to be seen.

Kathy turned the hat over and over in her hands. It was made of heavy wool felt, flexible but sturdy. Grimy fingerprints darkened the brim where Kate had habitually touched it. Inside the crown she found a small leather sticker that said *Producto de Buenos Aires* in shiny gold letters.

Just for fun, she clapped the hat over her own short curls. It fit perfectly. It smelled like peanuts and cigars and sweet green grass.

Kathy smiled and stuck her hands in her pockets, wondering how far away New York City was.

Last But Not Least

Robert J. Sawyer

Matt stood in the field on the bitter October morning. The wind's icy fingers reached right through Matt's skin to chill his bones. It was crazy that Mr. Donner made them wear their gym shorts on a day like today — but if Donner had any compassion in him, any humanity, any kindness at all, Matt had never seen it.

"I'll take Spalding."

"Gimme Chen."

Last week, Matt had tried to get out of phys. ed. class by pretending he'd lost his gym shorts; he'd put his own shorts in the school's lost and found. But Donner had an extra pair he lent him — and he said that if Matt showed up without shorts again, he'd make him take the class in his underwear.

"I pick Oxnard."

"I'll take Modigliani."

Matt didn't mind being outdoors, and he didn't mind getting some exercise, but he hated phys. ed. — hated it as much as he hated it when his parents fought, when he had to go to the dentist, when that dog over on Parkhurst came chasing after him.

He knew he was scrawny, knew he was uncoordinated. But did he have to be humiliated because of it? Made to feel like a total loser?

"Johnson."

"Peelaktoak."

There were twenty-four boys in Matt's gym class. Today they were playing soccer. But it didn't matter what the sport was; it always worked the same way. Mr. Donner would pick two students to be captains.

And then the ritual would begin.

"Gimme Van Beek."

"Takahashi."

The captains would take turns picking from the other students to create the two teams.

Matt understood the sick, evil logic of it all: twenty-four kids wasn't a big group. If you just took the first dozen alphabetically and made them one team, and had the second dozen be the other team, you might end up with two unevenly matched sides.

But this way . . .

This humiliating, mortifying way . . .

This way supposedly ensured fairness, supposedly made sure that the teams would be equal, made sure that the game would be exciting, that everyone would have a good time.

Everyone except those who were picked last, that is.

"Becquerel."

"Bergstrom."

Matt's big brother, Alf, was in law school. Alf said students fought hard for ranking in their classes. If you got the highest mark — if you finished first — you'd get a million-dollar contract from a huge law firm. If you finished last, well, Alf said maybe it would be time to think about another career. The stress on Alf was huge; Matt could see that every time his brother came home for a weekend. But Alf had chosen that stress, had chosen to be judged and ranked.

But phys. ed. wasn't something Matt had decided he wanted to take; he *had* to take it. Whether he liked it or not, he had to subject himself to this torture.

"Bonkowski."

Matt was the only one left now, and Cartwright, the other captain, didn't even bother to call out his name. Cartwright's rolled eyes said it all: he wasn't picking Matt Sinclair – he just happened to be the last guy left.

Matt blew out a heavy sigh. It was cold enough that he could see his breath form a frosty cloud.

Science class. The class Matt excelled in.

"And the process by which plants convert sunlight into food is called . . . ?" Mr. Pope looked out at the students, sitting in pairs behind black-topped lab desks.

Matt raised his hand.

"Yes, Matthew?"

"Photosynthesis," he said.

"That's right, Matthew. Very good. Now, although they both undergo photosynthesis, there are two very different types of trees. There are evergreens and the other kind, the kind that loses its leaves each fall. And that kind is called . . . ?"

Matt's hand shot into the air again.

"Anybody besides Matthew know?" asked Mr. Pope.

Blank faces all around. Matt smiled to himself. Why don't we arrange all the students in here, putting them in order of how intelligent they are? Take the smartest person first – which, well, gee, that would be Matt, of course – then the next smartest, then the one after that, right down to . . . oh, say, down to Johnson over there. Johnson was always an early pick in gym class, but if we made selections here in science class, he'd be the one left until the end every time.

"All right," said Mr. Pope, "since no one else seems to know, Matthew, why don't you enlighten your classmates?"

"Deciduous," Matt said proudly.

"Browner," whispered the girl behind him. And "Brainiac," said Eddy Bergstrom, sitting at the next desk.

It wasn't fair, thought Matt. They cheer when someone makes a goal. Why can't they cheer when someone gets an answer right?

This time, things would be different. This time, Mr. Donner had selected Paul Chandler, Matt's best friend, to be one of the team captains.

Matt felt himself relaxing. For once in his life, he wouldn't be last.

Paul called out his first pick. Esaki – a good choice. Esaki wasn't the strongest guy in the class, but he was one of the most agile.

The other captain, Oxnard, made his initial selection: Ehrlich. An obvious pick – Ehrlich towered half a head above everyone else.

Paul again: "Gimme Spalding."

Well, that made sense. Spalding was the biggest bully in school. Paul *had* to pick him early on, lest he risk being beaten up on the way home.

Oxnard's turn: "I'll take Modigliani."

Paul: "Ng."

Paul was playing it cool; that was good. It wouldn't do to take Matt *too* early — everyone would know that Paul was choosing him just because they were best friends.

"Let me have . . . Vanier," Oxnard said.

Paul made a show of surveying the remaining students. "Papadatos," he said.

Matt's heart was beginning to sink. Paul couldn't humiliate him the way the others had. Surely he would pick him in the next round.

"Herzberg."

"Peelaktoak."

Or the round after that . . .

"Becquerel."

"Johnson."

Or . . .

"Van Beek."

"Dowling."

But no—

No, it was going to be the same as always.

Paul — his friend — had left him for last, just as everyone else always did.

Matt felt his stomach churning.

At lunch, Paul sat down opposite Matt in the cafeteria. "Hey, Matt," he said.

Matt focused all his attention on his sandwich — peanut butter and jelly on whole wheat, cut in half diagonally.

"Earth to Matt!" said Paul. "Helll-ooo!"

Matt looked up. He kept his voice low; he didn't want the others sitting nearby to hear. "Why didn't you pick me in gym class?"

"I *did* pick you," protested Paul.

"Yeah. Last."

Paul seemed to consider this, as if realizing for the first time that Matt might have taken his actions as a betrayal. "Hey, Matt-o, I'm sorry, man. But it was probably my only time getting to be a captain all year, you know? And I wanted a good team."

A miracle occurred.

Matt was picked – not for a team, not by one of his classmates. No, no – this was better. Much better. Matt was picked by Mr. Donner to be one of the team captains. The game today was football; Matt didn't know much about it, except that some of the other boys had snickered when he'd once referred to a gain of ten meters, instead of ten yards. In theory, they would be playing touch football, but in reality . . .

In reality, he still had scabs on his knees from the last time they'd played this game, when Spalding had tackled Matt, driving him to the ground, his skin shredding on a broken piece of glass hidden in the grass.

And once, last year, Matt had actually managed to tag the runner going by him, the guy clutching the football. Matt *had* touched him – he was sure he had. A good, clean connection between his hand and the other guy's shoulder. But the other player had continued on, ignoring the touch – denying it, denying Matt, as if to be touched by him would be an unbearable humiliation. The guy had run on into the end zone, doing the exaggerated victory dance he'd seen professional players do on TV. His teammates had demanded that Matt explain why he hadn't tagged the guy. He had protested that he had, of course, but no one had believed him.

The boys were all lined up in a row. Matt moved out in front of them, as did Takahashi, the other person Mr. Donner had tapped to be a captain.

Donner looked at the two captains, then, with a little shrug for the other boys, as if to convey that things were mismatched already, he said, "Matt, you choose first."

Matt surveyed the twenty-two remaining boys: different sizes and shapes, different colors of eyes and hair and skin, different temperaments, different aptitudes. None of them was foolish enough to say anything disparaging about Matt being chosen as a captain; they all wanted to be picked early on, and would do nothing to jeopardize that.

"Matt?" said Mr. Donner, prodding him to get on with it.

Matt continued to look at the faces in front of him. Either Esaki or Ehrlich would be a good choice, but—

No.

No, this was too good an opportunity to pass up. "Bonkowski," Matt called out.

There were some snickers. Little Leo Bonkowski, looking absolutely stunned at being chosen first, crossed over to stand next to Matt.

Takahashi wasted no time. "Ehrlich," he said. Kurt Ehrlich strutted over to stand next to Takahashi.

Matt's turn again. "Bergstrom," he said. Eddy Bergstrom was fat and clumsy. He moved over to stand with Matt.

"I'll take Esaki," said Takahashi.

The other obvious choice – Esaki was strong, and he studied martial arts in the evenings. He and Ehrlich were always the first two choices; Matt couldn't remember a time when they'd ended up on the same team.

Matt looked at the remaining boys. Sepp Van Beek was looking at the ground, oblivious to what was going on; Matt rather suspected he usually looked much the same way himself during the picking ritual. "Van Beek," he said.

Sepp didn't move; he hadn't been paying attention.

"Hey, Sepp!" Matt called out.

This time Van Beek did look up, astonished. He half-ran across to join Matt's team, a silly grin splitting his features.

"Singh," said Takahashi decisively. A burly fellow moved over to the other side.

"Modigliani," said Matt.

By now, it was obvious to everyone what Matt was up to: he was taking the least physically adept boys, the ones who were puny, or overweight, or awkward, or just plain gentle.

Takahashi frowned; his expression conveyed that he felt the upcoming game was going to be like taking candy from a baby. "Gimme Ng," he said.

Matt surveyed the dwindling pool of boys. "Chen."

Takahashi snorted, then: "Cartwright."

"Take Vanier," Modigliani said to Matt, distancing himself from the obvious lunacy of what Matt was doing.

But Matt shook his head and said, "Oxnard."

"Vanier," said Takahashi.

It was Matt's turn again. Now things were getting difficult. There were no truly bad players left – only interchangeably mediocre ones. The next logical choice might have been Spalding, the bully, but Matt would have rather played a man short than have Spalding on his team. At last, he said, "Dowling."

Takahashi wasn't one to miss an opportunity. "Spalding," he said at once.

"Finkelstein," said Matt.

"Papadatos."

There were only six boys left: Herzberg, Johnson, Peelaktoak, Becquerel, Collins, and . . .

And Paul Chandler.

Matt wondered whether he'd deliberately been avoiding choosing Paul, repayment for the indignity of last time. Perhaps. But the six remaining students were neither particularly good nor particularly bad. Maybe if Matt had paid more attention in gym class, he'd have some idea of how to rank them, but at this stage he really couldn't distinguish them on the basis of ability . . . or lack of it.

But he would not do to Paul what Paul had done to him. "Chandler," Matt called out.

Paul came running over, an expression of gratitude on his freckled face; normally, of course, he'd have been taken long before this. Maybe he did now understand what it felt like without Matt having to actually put him through it.

"Collins," said Takahashi.

Matt tried not to shrug visibly. "Peelaktoak."

"Herzberg," said Takahashi.

"Becquerel."

And Takahashi took the final boy: "Johnson."

Matt looked at his team, then at the other side. The two groups could not have been more mismatched. For the first time since he'd started making choices, Matt glanced over at Mr. Donner. He'd hoped to see a small, understanding smile on the gym teacher's angular face – an acknowledgment that he got it, that he understood what Matt was trying to say. But Mr. Donner was frowning, and shaking his head slowly back and forth in disapproval.

"We're going to be slaughtered," said Bonkowski to Matt as the two teams moved out onto the field.

It was a day of multiple miracles. Not only had Matt been chosen to be captain, but he even caught the ball about a minute into the game. He realized in panic that he had no idea which set of goalposts belonged to his team – the closer one, over by the road, or the farther one, by the fence that separated the schoolyard from the adjacent houses.

He had to pick one – had to make one more choice – and he needed to do it in a fraction of a second.

Matt chose the farther one. It would be a longer run, but there were fewer boys from either team deployed in that direction. He worked his legs as hard as he could, pumping them up and down like pistons. What a glorious victory it would be if the weaker team actually won the game! And if he – Matthew Sinclair! – got a . . . a *touchdown*, it was called – well, then, that would put an end to his being chosen last!

He ran and ran and ran, as fast as he could. His feet pounded into the sod, still damp from the morning dew. He thought, or imagined at least, that clods of dirt were flying up from his footfalls as he ate up meter after meter – no, no, no – yard after yard, coming closer and closer to the goal line. His lungs were aching from gulping in so much cold air, and his heart felt as though it would burst within his chest. But if he could only—

Ooof!

A hand had slammed into his back – he'd been touched!

No! It was unfair! He *deserved* this chance, this opportunity, but—

But the rules were clear: this was touch football, and Matt had to stop running now.

But he couldn't – for it had been more than a touch; it had been a good, firm shove, a push impelling him on.

He found himself pitching forward, the moist grass providing little traction. And the boy who had pushed him from behind was now slamming into him, as if he, too, were sliding on the slick turf. But Matt knew in an instant that that wasn't it; oh, it was supposed to look like an accident, but he was really being tackled.

Matt slammed into the ground, so hard that he thought the football, crushed beneath his chest, would actually pop open. The other boy – Spalding it was; he could see that now – slammed down on top of him. Almost at once, a third boy – Captain Takahashi himself – piled on top.

The sound of Mr. Donner's whistle split the air, but belatedly, as if he'd been reluctant to interrupt good theater, to bring an end to just punishment. But the whistle was ignored. Matt's crime of creating mismatched teams was too great. Somebody shouted out, "Pile on!" Another body slammed on top of them, and one more after that, and then—

Crrrackkk!

It was an incredible, heart-stopping sound, like a gunshot. If Matt hadn't been buried under so many bodies, he expected he would have heard it echo off the school's brick walls.

There was a moment of nothingness, of no sensation, while the other boys reacted to the sound.

And then—

And then pain, incredible pain, indescribable pain.

The agony coursed through Matt's body, starting in his leg, shooting up his spine, assaulting his brain.

The other boys, sensing something was deeply wrong, began to climb off. As their weight shifted on top of Matt, fresh, fiery pain sliced through him.

At last, Spalding got up. Matt looked up and saw an expression on the bully's face he'd never seen before: a look of fear, of horror. Spalding was staring at Matt's right leg.

Matt swung his head down to have a look himself, and . . .

For a moment, he thought he was going to vomit. The sight was horrifying, unnatural.

Matt's right thigh was *bent* in the middle, twisted in a hideous way. He reached down and hiked up his gym shorts as far as they would go, so he could see—

God, no.

His thighbone – his *femur*, as he'd gladly have told Mr. Pope – was clearly broken. The bone was pushed up toward the surface, pressing against the skin, as if any second now it would burst out, a skeletal eruption.

Matt stared at it a few seconds more, then looked up. Mr. Donner had arrived by now, panting slightly, and Matt saw him looming above. "Don't move, Matt," he said. "Don't move."

Matt enjoyed the look on the teacher's face – one of incredible unease. There would be an inquiry, of course; Donner would be in the hot seat. And the faces of the other boys were equally satisfying: eyes wide in fear or revulsion, mouths hanging loosely open.

Matt opened his own mouth.

And a sound emerged – but not the sound the other boys might have expected. Not a scream, not a wail of pain, not the sound of crying.

No. As Matt looked down at his twisted leg again, he began to laugh, a throaty sound, starting as a bizarre chuckle and then growing louder and more raucous.

He looked back up at the other boys – his teammates, his tormentors – and he continued to laugh.

Some of the boys were backing slowly away now, their faces showing their confusion, their wariness. The damaged leg was bad enough, but this inappropriate laughter was just too darned *creepy*. They'd always known Sinclair was a little weird, but they'd never have said he was crazy. . . .

They don't get it, thought Matt. They don't get it at all. He'd snapped his leg playing football! How cool was that! It was a badge of honor, and people would talk about it for years: Matt Sinclair, the guy whose leg got broken on the – yes, he knew the word; it came to him – on the *gridiron*.

And there was more – wonderfully more. Matt's brother, Alf, had broken his leg once, falling off a ladder; Matt knew what was going to happen. He'd have to wear a cast for weeks, or even months. Yes, that would be uncomfortable; yes, it would be awkward. But he welcomed it, because it meant that at least for a while, he would be excused from the horrors of phys. ed.

That reprieve would be great, but things would be fine after the cast was removed too. For when he eventually came back to gym class, Matthew Sinclair, football hero, knew he would never be picked last again.

In the Heart of November

Scott Nicholson

Margaret sat on the tombstone, swinging her legs. Ellen could read Margaret's name carved in the gray granite, though the letters were blurred.

"How long have we been friends?" Margaret asked, her voice like a lost wind.

"You mean . . . before or after?" Ellen pulled her sweater more tightly across her chest. The graveyard was in the heart of November, all shadow and chill and flapping brown leaves.

"Both, silly."

"Seven years."

"And have I ever broken a promise or blabbed a secret?"

Ellen looked away. Even though Margaret was almost invisible, her eyes glowed bright and strange. Ellen had stopped by the graveyard every day after school since her best friend had been buried, and they often spent hours out here in the summer, talking about boys and Ellen's mom and Mrs. Deerfield's geometry tests. Margaret knew more of Ellen's secrets than anybody.

"I don't know," Ellen said. "You never blab on this side, but you could be telling my secrets to every dead person in the world for all I know."

Margaret's wispy features darkened. "Dead people don't care about your problems. They've got their own."

"Their problems can't be as bad as mine."

Margaret drifted down from the tombstone and put a cold hand on Ellen's shoulder. "I wish you would never have to find out."

"If I were dead, then it wouldn't matter if boys treated me like I was dirt."

"Don't be so sure."

"Do boys like you . . . over *there*?" Ellen tried to picture Doug as a ghost but couldn't. He was too tall and healthy and strong. He was meant to be running up and down a soccer field, as swift as sunshine, his dark curly hair flying about his face.

"Dead boys just aren't very interesting," Margaret said. "They don't want to do anything but sleep."

Margaret put her hands together, and the pale fingers merged. "It's hard to hold hands when you don't have much to hang on to. And kissing . . ." Margaret puckered her lips and made an exaggerated smacking sound. "Nobody likes cold lips."

"Gross," said Ellen.

Margaret's giggle spilled out over the grass and echoed off the stone wall that surrounded the cemetery. The sun was sinking into the gnarled tops of the trees. Cars passed by the highway beyond the wall, the wheels making whispers on the asphalt.

"I'd better get home," Ellen said. "Mom will be mad."

"I wish you could stay here all the time."

"But you don't want me to be dead."

"I just get lonely sometimes. Lonely for living people. I miss being alive."

Ellen looked into Margaret's unearthly eyes. "You miss Doug."

"Wouldn't you?"

Ellen didn't say anything. How could she tell her best friend that they were in love with the same guy? She'd hoped Margaret would get over him. Margaret and Doug didn't have anything in common anymore, especially now.

But they had been close once. Back in the seventh grade, they'd been as steady as anybody. And all Ellen could do was watch with envy as they held on to each other at school dances or talked quietly during lunch or passed notes in class. After Margaret was hit by a car and killed, Ellen thought Doug was going to die as well, only from a broken heart instead of a broken body.

"I've got to go," Ellen said. Her mom would yell at her for being late again. If only Mom knew that the more she yelled, the more Ellen wanted to be late. Ellen waved and started through the rows of tombstones.

Margaret followed. "I may come out tomorrow," she said.

Ellen turned, chilled by more than just the long shade of a dead oak. "I thought they didn't like it when you come out."

"Who cares what they think?" Margaret shook her see-through hair. "I get tired of them telling me what to do and where to go. They don't want anybody to have any fun."

Ellen didn't know who "they" were, but Margaret's eyes always narrowed with anger when she spoke of them. "You aren't supposed to leave," Ellen said.

"Gosh, you're starting to sound like your mom." Margaret's hollow voice rose in pitch as she mimicked Ellen's mom.

"'You were *supposed* to be home an hour ago. You were *supposed* to make an A on that math test.'"

Ellen laughed, even though Margaret's shrill imitation was too perfect and it reminded Ellen of what was waiting at home. "What will they do to you if you leave?"

Margaret shrugged. "You don't want to know."

Margaret had left the cemetery once, had floated outside Ellen's window in the mobile-home park. This had been about two weeks after her burial. Margaret had seemed so much more lost, lonely, and *creepy* outside of the graveyard. Whatever invisible chains kept her bound to the dirt under her tombstone must have been painful to break, because when Ellen visited the next day, Margaret had faded to nearly nothing. A month passed before Margaret returned to her usual thin form.

Ellen moved to her best friend and gave her a hug. At least, she tried to. Her arms passed through Margaret, raising goosebumps. "Don't do anything to make them mad. They might take you forever next time."

"I want to see Doug," Margaret said.

"Doug's not worth it."

"How do you know? What do *you* know about losing somebody you love?"

Ellen's eyes grew hot with held tears. Margaret was beautiful. She could have had any boy she wanted. Ellen was afraid that Margaret still could, even dead. "I've really got to go."

"I'm sorry. I wasn't trying to be mean."

Ellen sniffled. "It's not your fault. I'm just feeling sorry for myself."

"See you tomorrow?"

Ellen nodded and hurried from the graveyard, making sure no one was looking before she climbed over the cemetery wall. She slipped into the woods and onto the well-worn path that led home.

"What's wrong?" Mom asked. "You've hardly eaten a bite. You're not going to starve yourself so you can look like the girls in *Seventeen*, are you? I told you to quit wasting money on those stupid magazines."

"No, Mom, I'm not on a diet." Ellen was tired of eating macaroni and cheese and greasy hamburgers. Mom's cooking made even the school cafeteria lunches look good.

"You look pale." Mom leaned over the small table and pressed her hand to Ellen's forehead. Her hand was nearly as cold as Margaret's. "You're not taking sick, are you?"

"I feel fine." Except her belly was like a nest of snakes. She was worried that Margaret would come out tomorrow.

"Well, you don't *look* fine."

"I think I just want to go lie down for a while."

"Got your homework done?"

Ellen nodded. She always did her homework while the teachers were explaining it to the rest of the class. Margaret may have had beauty, but Ellen was lucky with books. Too bad Doug was smart, too, and never asked Ellen to help him with his homework.

"Well, good. That's one less thing I've got to worry about." Mom's face was pinched and tired, her cheeks flushed. She might have been drinking. Ellen couldn't smell anything over the cloying aroma of cheese powder.

Ellen pushed her plate away, knowing she'd see the left-overs again tomorrow. And tomorrow might bring other horrors. She went down the narrow paneled hall to her bedroom. The bed took up most of the floor, and she crawled onto it and lay on her back, looking at the pictures of musicians and unicorns on her walls. The unicorns would have to go. She was getting too old for unicorns.

She reached over, slid her desk drawer open, and took out the photograph. Its edges were worn from handling, but the face was just as wonderful as always. Doug smiled out from between the white borders, straight teeth and dark eyes and curly hair. Something swished against the window, and Ellen's breath froze in her lungs. What if Margaret was at her window, looking in? What if Margaret had seen her gazing longingly at Doug's picture?

She got on her knees and looked out the window. The lights blazed in the windows of the other mobile homes, which were arranged as awkwardly as tombstones. Different sizes, moved in at different times, all slowly fading under the wear of time. This was her graveyard, and she was as trapped here as Margaret was in the graveyard of grass and granite and artificial flowers.

Nobody stirred outside, neither the dead nor the living. Leaves scurried across the bare yards like frantic mice. A pole at the end of the park glowed with a sick blue light, but it was too cold and weak to attract bugs. Ellen drew her curtains tight and rested back on her pillow.

Doug. He'd said hello to her in the hall the other day. She summoned the memory in all its glory: the flash of his eyes, the warm tone of his voice, his head above the crowd of students changing class. She'd been too nervous to say anything in response. All she could do was give a lame wave and what she hoped was a smile.

Probably looked like a grimace. She brought a small hand mirror from her drawer and practiced her smile. Dimples that were dumpy instead of cute. Her cheeks were fat. She had a pimple on her chin. God, she was *hideous*. No wonder Doug didn't want her.

She and Doug had been close briefly, right after Margaret's death. They had sat together at lunch, Doug wearing sunglasses so that no one could tell that Mr. Cool had been crying. They'd even hugged at the funeral, and now Ellen embraced that fleeting memory of his muscles.

If only Margaret could die every day, then maybe Doug and I—

As soon as she had the thought, she was sickened. She'd rather have Margaret back alive than have any guy in the world. Anyway, if Margaret were alive, Doug would still be going out with her. Margaret had been beautiful. Still was. And Ellen was a frumpy, dumpy piece of nobody. She cried herself to a restless sleep.

"You didn't come out," Ellen said the next afternoon.

Margaret lowered her voice, looked around at the other graves. "I was scared."

"I don't blame you." Ellen felt a small spark of joy, a lightness in her chest. If Margaret didn't come out, everything would be okay.

"I want to see him."

"You'd better be careful, Margaret."

"I don't have to talk to him or anything. I just want to *see* him. To remember what he's like."

"What about Doug?" Ellen asked. "What if you freak him out?"

"I didn't freak *you* out."

"Well, you did a little at first. I mean, it's not like I believed in ghosts or anything, or did one of those corny seances to try to bring you back."

"I wonder if Doug misses me as much as I miss him."

Ellen didn't know whether to lie or not. She had never kept secrets from Margaret before. She looked at the ground, at the seam of stubborn dirt where the grass hadn't taken root.

"Are you ashamed of having me for a friend?" Margaret asked.

"Of course not." Ellen knelt in the moist grass by the tombstone. "You'll always be my best friend. Forever."

"Better than Doug?"

Does she know? Ellen's throat was tight. What would a ghost do to you if you tried to steal her boyfriend?

"Doug still thinks about you a lot," Ellen managed to say, which wasn't a lie. "I talked to him a few weeks ago. He said that you guys listened to Crash Test Dummies together. He said that 'Swimming in Your Ocean' was your favorite song."

"Crash Test Dummies. Now *that's* what I call irony, given the way I got killed."

Ellen tried to change the subject away from Doug and death. "Do they have music . . . over there?"

Margaret looked beyond the graveyard, beyond trees and stone and all things solid, as if she hadn't heard Ellen. "It doesn't hurt to get killed. It hurts more afterward. Being dead, I mean. And knowing it. That's the worst thing."

"I wish I could trade places with you." So Doug would be in love with *her*. Even if she couldn't do anything about it, couldn't hold his hand or kiss him. She'd be happy enough just to know he carried her in his heart. Just to be able to make him happy or sad when he thought of her.

"Don't say that." Margaret drifted down from the stone. Part of her misty flesh seeped across Ellen's face. Ellen shivered.

"It hurts to be dead, Ellen. It hurts to remember everything you lost."

"You haven't lost me," Ellen said, wondering if Margaret was splashing the chill of death on her face just to warn her. But Ellen would never commit suicide. She was too scared. And if she died, she'd never have Doug. But would Doug have *her*?

"I don't ever want to lose you." Margaret's smile was a white sliver of movement among the smoky threads of her face. The front gate of the cemetery creaked open.

"Somebody's coming," Ellen said, but Margaret had already disappeared, back to her cold and dreamless sleep. Ellen pretended to mumble a prayer in case the visitors happened to see her. Then she went out the front gate and headed toward the soccer field.

Ellen's mom would be mad, but Ellen didn't care. Nothing else mattered anymore. Let everybody else hate her. She had to find out once, for all, and forever.

"This is really weird, Ellen," Doug said.

What did Doug know about weirdness? His world was soccer games, shooting for college scholarships, getting tons of pictures in the yearbook. He'd been in the graveyard before, but not since Margaret's funeral and certainly never when the sky was purple with sundown. A pale slice of moon hung in bare branches like an ornament.

"How come you've never been back?" Ellen asked.

"Because I . . ." Doug paused, gasped. "I don't know. It makes me think about her, and I don't like to think about her. It makes my chest hurt."

They stood before Margaret's grave, Doug shivering in his soccer shorts and T-shirt. She'd dragged him here right after practice, had called him to the sidelines and told him she had something really important to show him. So important it couldn't wait for him to get dressed.

She'd taken his hand, and he hadn't pulled away. She led him across the street and over the hill, feeling the eyes of Doug's friends on her back. They probably thought good old Doug was going to score, put another one in the net. Ellen trembled as they walked, brushing aside his questions until they came to the graveyard.

"Margaret is my best friend," Ellen said. Doug looked at her as if she were crazy, but she didn't feel crazy at all. In fact, for the first time in years, she felt that her life was under her own control.

"Yeah, Margaret was great," Doug said, looking around at the tombstones, gray in the weak light. "She was really special."

"I have to know, Doug. Did you really love her?"

Doug let go of her hand. "You're scaring me."

"The truth is nothing to be afraid of." Ellen squinted at Margaret's grave but could see none of the strange milkiness of her ghost. She hoped that they hadn't called Margaret away, that they hadn't confined her to some dismal, dark hibernation. *"Did you love her?"*

Doug looked around. He seemed uncomfortable without an audience. Ellen wondered if this was how he acted when he was alone with Margaret. "Uh, yeah. Sure. Of course I did."

"How many girls have you gone out with since then?"

"What's that got to do with anything?"

"It's got everything to do with everything."

"Are you feeling okay?"

"I'm fine." Ellen grinned, not caring if her dimples were dumpy. "Never been better. How many girls?"

"Heck, I don't know. Five, six."

"Maybe ten?"

"Maybe."

"And you loved Margaret the best?"

"You're weird. I've got to go."

"Just answer me, and then you can leave."

He scratched his head. His eyes reflected the moonlight. "Well, I loved her. But you've got to move on. You've got to keep living. I know you were her best friend, but I didn't know you were so hung up on her."

"Even dead people have feelings." She almost wished Margaret would rise like fog to tell Doug how much she missed him. Ellen wondered how Mr. Cool would handle *that*.

"I'm getting out of here."

Doug headed for the gate, hunched, his arms huddled across his chest. November was always cold, especially in the graveyard. But Ellen knew some things were colder than November. Like a guy's heart.

"She loved you, you know," Ellen called.

Doug stopped near the gate, his shadow mingling with the wrought-iron bars. "I thought you were taking me out here so we could be alone. I was going to kiss you. I was going to be gentle. I was even going to walk you home after."

"I bet you say that to all the girls," Margaret said, her voice everywhere and nowhere.

Doug glanced at the sky, shook his head as if to clear away cobwebs or memories or imagined voices, then hurried through the gate.

"He's not so hot after all," Margaret said from her tombstone perch. "Not like I remember him."

Ellen turned, wondering how long Margaret had been sitting there. "Some people grow on you, and some don't."

"You could have fallen in love with him," Margaret said. "I wouldn't have minded too much."

"I know. But every time I kissed him, I would have thought of you. And he wouldn't have."

"Yeah." The moon shone into Margaret, making her hair radiant. She was beautiful, both inside and out. "Well, when you're dead, warm lips are gross anyway."

They shared a laugh, and even though the wind howled around them, Ellen was warm. She might not know what losing love was like, but she knew what *having* it was like.

"You'd better get home," Margaret said. "Your mom's going to kill you."

"Naw. She's not going to kill me. I'm going to live a long time."

The cemetery was silent except for the brittle rattling of bone-dry leaves. After a moment, Margaret said, "Live for both of us, okay?"

Ellen reached out, held the wispy hand of her best friend. "I promise," she whispered.

Ellen left Margaret to her dark sleep and headed for the gate, street, and home. Tomorrow Doug would be telling half the school that she was nuts, but she didn't care. Doug could go stuff himself as far as she was concerned. She could hardly wait to get home and tear his picture into shreds.

There was one more thing. She paused at the gate. "See you tomorrow, Margaret," she called across the empty graveyard.

A peaceful hush was her only answer.

The iBook

Tim Wynne-Jones

It was Chater's first heist. He knew Slack would be watching him to see if he freaked, to see if he wet himself. They were always testing; it was worse than school, but the rewards were higher.

He wasn't frightened – hadn't he proven that? Treating that Gap brat Jer Tolstoy to a fat lip outside the arcade: that was his audition. That's what had caught Slack's eye. Chater was ready for anything.

He stole things – who didn't? – but he had never done a house, a B&E. And he'd chosen just the right place for his debut. It was his present to Slack and the gang.

"It's out in Bliss Valley," he said.

Slack sniggered. "That's tree-hugger territory. What're we gonna lift, a sack of granola?"

The others laughed.

"How 'bout a basket-load of Grateful Dead records?" said Sub-Total.

Chater despised Sub-Total, but he kept his peace, stared

the laughter down, watched the interest swim back into Slack's rheumy eyes.

"So what's the deal?" said Slack, relaxing his sneer a notch or two.

"Lister Strang," said Chater. Just that. It was all he needed to say.

"The writer guy?" said Sub-Total.

Chater didn't bother to nod, didn't bother to look at the underling. Of course, the writer guy. Author of *Beat Red*, *Kill Joy*, *Hell's Teeth*, *Strang Bedfellows*, *Beast Friends*, and a whole gorefest of other thick novels of terror.

"Like we're gonna hit some place in Hollywood," said Blink.

Chater rolled his eyes. "The dude lives right here under your pimply nose. Believe me."

"Well, I don't," said Blink. "How come we never heard about it?"

Chater wanted to say, "Because you're stupid," but again he restrained himself. "Because he craves anonymity," he said. Chater liked saying that. He wanted Slack to know he was smart.

Slack didn't look impressed. "And his place is gonna be, like, electronic-surveillance city, man: lasers, barbed wire, maybe a couple of underfed Dobermans."

Chater had expected this response. He smiled a long, slow, sly smile. "Didn't I tell you I cased the place, watched his movements? I thought I told you that." Then he took something out of the pocket of his fake leather jacket and laid it ceremoniously in Slack's hand. It was a gold lighter with the name Strang etched on its side in Gothic letters. "Just walked in," said Chater. "Wanna check my leg for teeth marks?"

Slack ignored the jibe, turned the lighter over in his hand a couple of times before pocketing it.

"You see, Strang can't stand the high-pitched sound of an alarm system," said Chater. "And he don't hold with locks. He says: 'I am not afraid of anything except what is inside my own head.'"

Slack didn't look impressed – he looked downright suspicious. "Where'd you hear that?" he said, pressing his nose up close to Chater's face. His breath stunk. He's already half-decayed, thought Chater.

"None of your business," he said.

Slack supplied the van, a puke yellow rustbucket stolen just for the job. He would also supply the fence. It was no use making a heist if you had nowhere to take the goods, nowhere to cash in.

Chater didn't expect to be with Slack very long. These guys were losers. But he needed to learn who was who. You had to start somewhere. He had a good mind, an active mind. How many teachers, guidance counselors, youth workers had told him that? Well, he was about to put that mind to work.

The house was huge and, as he had promised, undefended. They backed the van right up to the ample front porch and started in. It was a treasure trove. Sub-Total giggled like a fool until Slack slapped him one.

He looked jumpy. It surprised Chater. Slack jostled him out of the way as he hurled a Persian rug into the van.

"Lighten up," said Chater. "Strang isn't coming back for hours."

Slack sniffed, rubbed his hands on his jeans. He gazed down the long, curving driveway toward the dirt road. "I don't like it," he muttered, then he darted back in for another load.

"Is he always this nervous?" Chater asked Sub-Total as they carted an eighty-inch Hitachi down the stairs.

Sub-Total shook his head. "He's usually cool as an outhouse toilet seat."

The truck filled up quickly. Everything was late model, top of the line. Chater doubted the gang had ever made such a good haul. So where was the respect? All he was getting from Slack were wary glances.

They had just about cleaned out the upstairs, but Chater was looking for something he hadn't yet found. He climbed a ladder on the second floor that led to a loft tucked under the pinnacle of the steeply sloping roof. He couldn't find the light switch, but the crowded shadows made him think, Bingo!

"Hey, give me a hand," yelled Slack from below. Chater found him in a spare bedroom tearing the wires out of a desktop computer. It wasn't much – Chater could tell at a glance – an old IBM clone.

"He must be keeping this for sentimental reasons," said Chater, smirking.

"Just shut up!" shouted Slack, shoving the monitor into Chater's gut. The edge was all that was left of Slack's voice.

"It's junk," said Chater. "But I think I know where its mother may be hiding," he added. Slack made a shut-yer-trap fist at him. Chater dropped the monitor at his feet.

Slack stared at it. Then he glared at Chater.

"Pick it up," he said in a hoarse whisper. Chater shook his head. Slack pushed by him and headed for the stairs with the printer and keyboard under his arms.

Junk, thought Chater, shaking his head. He didn't pick up the monitor. He headed for the loft. He'd show them. A writer like Strang would have some big-time equipment with all the add-ons: tons of memory, Zip drives, laser printer, scanner . . .

He made his way by touch and moonlight through the crowded shadows. It was an office, just as he had guessed: filing cabinets, bookshelves, boxes. But with deepening surprise and annoyance, Chater discovered that there seemed to be no trace of technology, no machine bigger than a pencil sharpener. Then he reached the desk, which sat directly under a tall window pointed at the top. It made him feel uncomfortable, as if he were in some nighttime church. The desk was vast, uncluttered, but square in the middle of the moonglow sat a small orange-and-white plastic case. It looked like some Fisher Price toy. That's what the others would have thought. Chater rubbed his hands together. He knew better. He sat down at the author's swivel chair and found the button to open the toy.

"Think Different," he muttered to himself, chuckling at the joke. For it was, as he had guessed, a laptop computer, the latest thing from Apple, the iBook.

Just then, he heard the van's engine sputter to life. He jumped up and stared out the window. The van was pulling away from the house. He brought his fists down hard on the desktop and bellowed with rage. The van fishtailed out onto the road and in a moment was lost to sight behind a wall of trees.

"This is my heist!" yelled Chater. "Mine!"

He got hold of himself, made himself sit down again. The quietness of the empty house settled around him. He sat with his back ramrod straight, as if he were the boss in some gangster flick, about to make an executive decision. He laid his hands on the desk to either side of the computer.

They'll be in town tomorrow like always, he told himself.

He would get what he had coming to him. No sweat. Then he looked down at the iBook and grinned. And this would be his little secret. This was all his.

He had to walk out to the highway. It was October cold, took him half an hour. Then it was another twenty minutes before some hayseed picked him up. Chater had stuffed the iBook into a black cloth sack he'd found in Strang's vestibule. If the hayseed was curious about the contents of the bag, he kept it to himself. The old Impala's fan was pumping out heat, the radio was pumping out country. Chater closed his eyes in defense.

"Hoo-wee," said the hayseed, slowing down all of a sudden. "Will you look at that, eh?"

Chater had drifted off for a moment. He opened his eyes. Up ahead lights were flashing, police were redirecting traffic. A roadblock! Automatically, he reached for the door handle. Then he saw the ambulance. There had been a crash. Picked out by spotlights were the remains of a puke yellow van wrapped around a telephone pole.

Chater lived up a long, dim, cat-piss stairway above Handy's Hardware downtown. When he was at last in his room with the door locked, he started laughing hysterically. He couldn't stop himself. He threw himself in the ratty chair by the window, his arms wrapped around the bag with the iBook inside. The laughter died, and he found he was shivering like a puppy. He clung to his prize.

Some debut.

Almost nothing had gone right. Slack had lost his nerve. The gang had blown it, lost everything. But not Chater. He summoned up a superior smile.

He pulled the iBook from its bag. He flipped the switch on the floor lamp beside the chair and examined the computer all over. It was tangerine orange in color. "My family number is M2453," he read on the back. "I was assembled in Taiwan." Cute.

He popped it open and stared with delight at the clear plastic keypad. Beautiful. His finger itched to give it a whirl. He had seen the ads, but as far as he knew this computer wasn't even on the market yet. So how did Lister Strang get a hold of one? Easy. Apple probably sent him one for free. Some kind of promo gimmick.

He pressed the Power button, and the screen came to life. Only one folder icon appeared. It was labeled "Stories." Chater clicked it open. In the folder, there was only one story, a short one, he thought, seeing that it used up only 13K of memory. But then he wondered if it was a story at all, because it was called "The iBook." Maybe it was some kind of instructional information. He clicked it open and started to read.

> *It was my first heist. I knew Slack would be watching me to see if I freaked, to see if I wet myself. They were always testing, it was worse than school, but the rewards were higher. . . .*

Chater sat back in stunned silence, his arms limp at his side. He squeezed his eyes shut, willing the text on the screen to change, to evaporate. But it wouldn't go. After a moment, he scrolled down to the end of the text – there were just over seven pages.

*But then I wondered if it was a story at all, because it was
called "The iBook." Maybe it was some kind of instructional
information. I clicked it open and started to read. . . .*

He was obviously losing it, hallucinating. It had been a
long night. He closed the document, closed the file. Then,
with a shaking hand, he dragged the file down to the trash-
can icon at the bottom of the screen. The trash can got fat.
Two more quick operations and it was thin again, the story
committed to cyber-oblivion. He switched off the iBook,
closed it, and stumbled to his unmade bed, where he fell, too
exhausted to even kick off his shoes.

There was a crowd at the arcade at noon the next day.
Everyone was gathered around Jer Tolstoy. He was playing
Tekken II. Chater shoved his way through the crowd. He liked
the way Jer flinched when he saw him coming, the way he lost
control of his fighter. On the screen, Eddy got creamed.

"Wassup?" Chater asked. But before Jer could talk,
someone in the crowd piped up.

"It's Slack, man. He's dead."

Chater looked around. Everyone was nodding his head.

"It's true," said Jer. "My dad was working emerge last night
when they brought him in."

Chater tried to keep his cool. "What about the others?"
he asked. It was a stupid thing to say. Jer picked up on it
right away.

"Who said anything about others?" he asked.

Chater shrugged, stuck his hands in his back pocket, Mr.
Couldn't-care-less. "I meant those deadbeats who were
attached to Slack's key chain."

"Sub-Total's in hospital," said Jer. "Dad thinks maybe he oughta do a brain transplant on him." There was a round of nervous laughter that ended soon enough when Chater grabbed Jer by his shirt front. Jer pushed his hands away. "Blink's in the can," he added with a menacing glare, as if to say, "And that's where you're heading, buddy." Then he turned back to his video game and fired it up with a couple of quarters. Chater muscled his way back through the crowd and headed for the door. The whispers followed him out onto the street.

He would have rather not run into Michelle. She was just coming out of Perks with a couple of school friends in tow. They fell back, sharing a look of disgust, as she advanced on him – he was a bad boy, not one of them, not in school. Chater wasn't fooled. They were secretly envious of her. He could see it in their eyes.

"A terrible thing has happened," said Michelle. She had her hand on his arm.

"So I hear," he said. He fought the urge to shake her off. He had got what he wanted out of her. Her father had been Strang's real-estate agent, and Michelle had a big mouth once you got her primed. Not that he had minded priming her, but that was then.

"Luckily, he got everything back," she said.

"What?" said Chater, caught off guard. "Who?"

"Mr. Strang," said Michelle. "He was robbed, Chater. Can you imagine? I hope he doesn't move away. God! It's so exciting having him as a neighbor. I mean, like . . . it's amazing."

Chater's mind was elsewhere. "He got everything back?"

"*Everything*," said Michelle. "Dad says it's nothing short of a miracle. Dad says that man has got powerful forces on his side."

Chater was saved any further of Michelle's father's observations. Her friends dragged her back off to school. But one of them, the redhead, looked back at Chater over her shoulder. Temma or Gemma or something like that. Gemma – that was it. She wore a mask of distaste, but Chater saw something – a glint in her eye – that looked to him like an invitation to untie the strings of that mask. He winked at her and she turned away, but not hurriedly. It was her red Fiero they climbed into.

The wind picked up, the sky clouded over. Chater hung out all day picking up what gossip he could, avoiding his place just in case. It was cold. At two he parked himself in the greasy spoon across the street from Handy's, nursing a coffee and watching for any signs that his place was under surveillance. No one showed. But he didn't want to go home. Around three, he wandered off to find a newspaper.

"Bungled Robbery Ends Tragically," proclaimed the headline on page one of the local rag. Chater scanned the report quickly, holding his breath the whole time. Finally, he sighed with relief. It sounded like the case was closed. There was nothing about the cops looking for a fourth culprit. He reread the article more closely. He read the last paragraph three times.

> Remarkably, none of the stolen property was seriously damaged in the devastating crash. When reached for comment, Mr. Strang would only say, "No personal loss could have grieved me more than the death of this foolish boy." Mr. Strang, interrupted this morning while hurriedly packing for a business trip, took the time to add, eloquently, "The only thing missing from my home after this sad episode is my peace of mind."

Nothing missing? Chater shook his head. "Check your office, Strang," he muttered. Then he told himself that any guy who didn't notice he was short one hot new computer didn't deserve it in the first place. The rationalization, however, wasn't quite enough to dislodge the uneasy feeling stirring in his gut.

The iBook was right where he had hidden it that morning, in his closet. He threw the black bag aside and placed the laptop on the table. He opened it, booted it up. The folder icon was back.

He had trashed it the night before. He was sure of it. But it was back. He opened the folder. There was still only the one story, "The iBook," but now it was 39K long. He clicked it open; the story started out the same. He quickly scrolled to the end.

> *I clicked it open; the story started out the same. I quickly scrolled to the end. . . .*

There was a flash of lightning outside! The lights in Chater's apartment flickered. But not the light on the screen before him. Before his eyes, the story was unfolding with Pentium speed, even as it happened.

> *Before my eyes, the story was unfolding with Pentium speed, even as it happened. . . .*

Roaring with fear and anger, Chater shoved the laptop away. It slid into a half-filled coffee mug, sent it crashing to the floor. He slammed the top down, jumped up, knocking over his chair. A long, low rumble of thunder ushered in the clamor of October rain. He stomped away from the table, then suddenly he was flying through the air, his feet entangled in the black bag. He landed hard on the floor and tore the strap from around his ankle, seething with rage, as if the bag were some rabid creature that had attacked him. He hurled it into a corner and clambered to his feet.

This is some kind of weird modem thing, he thought. He marched to the window. The rain was slashing down, the wind shook the glass in its frame, rainwater pooled on the stained and dusty sill. Chater scanned the bank of windows across the darkened street. He was looking for a watcher at a keyboard, but the windows were dark or curtained. He leaned his head against the glass and stared down at the greasy spoon across the way. There was no one in the steamy window. He scanned the parked cars on the street, looking for one with a writer at the wheel. Nothing. He banged the flat of his hand against the glass. "He's playing me!" he shouted at the night. "He's playing me."

Get a grip, he told himself a moment later. He crossed his arms on his chest. But suddenly unable to control himself, he rushed to the table, picked up the iBook, and hurled it with all his might. It smashed against the fridge and fell to the floor, landing open.

Chater sunk to his knees. He crawled toward the computer. He expected the screen to be shattered or, at the very least, blank. But the story had not stopped unfolding. Everything that had just happened was recorded there.

And more.

> *It was getting ahead of me, thinking thoughts before I could think them. I had to get rid of it — it was too hot to pawn, too dangerous to keep. I had to take it back. Yes! Take it back to Strang.*

"Wrong!" Chater hissed. He tucked the iBook under his arm and marched to the door of his apartment. At the rear end of the dim corridor was a window. Below it in the alley stood the hardware store's dumpster. Chater pulled up the sash, leaned out into the rain, and raised the laptop above his head. He was just about to let it fly when a thought froze him. The story. He had tried to dump it once without success. How much more successful was he going to be throwing it into this real trash can? If there was any chance of somebody finding the computer intact, opening it, reading what it had to say, he was dead meat. It would be Exhibit A for the prosecution.

Slowly, he closed the window and leaned, soaking wet, against it. Then he smiled grimly. What he needed was a hammer. A sledgehammer. Or just a good, big rock. He laughed out loud in the echoey hall, imagining the crisp plastic case shattering into a million tangerine-colored shards.

"How do you like the sound of that?" he shouted at the thing in his hands. Then he rolled his eyes. What was wrong with him! It didn't have teeth. The danger was all in his head. He wiped the rain from his face. Knowing that deliverance was only one heavy object away, Chater felt some of his natural sneering confidence return to him. But the feeling was shattered by the sound of his door buzzer.

He did not fall so much as crumple into the back corner of the hallway. But the buzzing was relentless, urgent, not to be denied. And now there was knocking. From the head of the steep stairs he saw, backlit by streetlight, the silhouette of the visitor at his door. It didn't look like the cops. The glass was pebbled, but he could see the impression of windblown hair, hair a lot longer than Michelle's. Gemma, he thought. Gemma *who had a car*.

In his room he pressed the button to let her in, then he found the crumpled black sack, thrust the iBook in it, and threw it on the bed. He raced to meet his uninvited guest. It was Gemma, all right. He could see in her eyes that the boldness that had brought her to him was wrestling with timidity, even suspicion. It made Chater feel cocksure, dangerous. It was a good feeling.

"I want to talk to you about Michelle," she said hesitantly, not quite able to meet his eyes. He could tell the line was rehearsed.

"No, you don't," he said, guiding her through his doorway. "You want to talk about us." But the smooth move was jarringly interrupted by the sound of the downstairs door opening again. There were no other roomers; it could only be Handy. "Make yourself at home," Chater said, and shutting the door behind him, he went down to cut his landlord off at the pass.

It took Chater a few minutes to calm the old man down, see him to the door, get rid of him. By the time he returned, Gemma was sitting on his unmade bed with the iBook open on her lap. She blushed when he came in and demurely lowered the screen.

He almost hit her, but he checked his anger, unclenched his fist and his throat. Waited for her response. When she returned her gaze to him, her eyes were glowing.

"I knew it," she said excitedly. "I knew you had some talent or something. I just never guessed you'd be so . . . so good."

Chater held his dread in check. "So now you know my secret," he said.

Gemma blushed again. Her chest was heaving. "You're a writer," she whispered. "That is so totally cool. I mean, I didn't read the whole story, just the last part—" She broke off, blushing.

"What part?" he asked gently, more curious than alarmed.

"The part about . . . about us," she said.

He sat down beside her on the bed and opened the screen.

> *From the head of the steep stairs I saw, backlit by streetlight,*
> *the silhouette of the visitor at my door. It didn't look like the*
> *cops. The glass was pebbled, but I could see the impression of*
> *windblown hair, hair a lot longer than Michelle's. Gemma.*
> *She had come to me, the answer to my prayers. I knew now*
> *I could go ahead with my plan; it would be all right. As long*
> *as Gemma was there, beside me.*

He could feel Gemma shuddering beside him. Then she said, hesitant again, uncertain. "Of course, it might not be you – I mean, you and me. The 'I' in the story doesn't have to be the author," she said. She giggled nervously.

Chater gazed at her suddenly, wide-eyed with surprise. It made her uncomfortable, as if maybe she had said something terminally stupid.

"All I meant was, like, I shouldn't assume because it's written in the first person that you really . . . you know, like me. I mean the 'I' could be anybody."

That's when Chater kissed her. How could he have been so stupid? There was nothing incriminating in the story. Nowhere in the text was his name mentioned. He scrolled back through it. Nowhere. He smiled a long, slow, sly smile. His good mind was active again.

It didn't take much to convince Gemma to drive him out to Lister Strang's. "He's sort of my teacher," he told her.

"Your mentor," she said breathlessly, her eyes fixed on the slippery road.

"Yeah, like that," he said. "I'm supposed to take him this story for him to . . . you know, comment on it."

"Oh, God," she said, grabbing his hand. "Can I meet him?"

Chater returned her hand to the wheel. "Maybe another time," said Chater. "He's pretty busy. I'm just gonna leave him the iBook."

"Why not a hard copy?"

But Chater's mind was working hard; he was way ahead of her. "Well, see, he makes his corrections right on the computer and then hands it back to me and I write some more."

Gemma's mouth was lolling open with wonder. "Kind of like a work-in-progress?"

Chater smiled. "Yeah, like that." Or a game, he thought. A game. And Strang had already told him his next move. *Take it back.* And that's what he was going to do.

Maybe he'd pick himself up a little memento on the way out, something easy to hawk, but he would exit light one headache, light one nightmare. Strang wasn't there; he had been "hurriedly packing" when the newspaper reporter had talked to him. There was no way there had been time for him to beef up his security system. Chater suspected that Strang wouldn't even have locked his door. Hadn't the author said he wasn't afraid of anything but what was in his head?

The great house stood in near total darkness. The door was not locked. Stealthily, Chater made his way to the second floor. He stood for a moment on the landing, listening to the dark. There was no sound but the gusting rain and his own shallow breathing. He climbed the ladder that led to the loft. There was no moon to guide him through the labyrinth of furniture to the desk under the window, but he found his way without difficulty. He sat in the swivel chair where, twenty-four hours ago, he had reveled in his discovery. In the driveway below Gemma waited; *she* would not drive off without him.

He placed the iBook back where he had found it and popped the lid. He clicked open the folder; the story was now all of 91K long. He was just going to open it for one last glance – to see how it ended – when he heard footsteps below. He froze. Then the desk lamp came on, making Chater gasp and fall back in his chair. The footsteps reached the ladder. Chater spun around. He jumped to his feet just as a head appeared in the gloom at the end of the loft. The dim light gleamed on a bald dome, then reflected off horn-rimmed glasses. Chater grabbed a heavy tape dispenser and stood ready to fight his way out. The man gained the loft, saw the stranger at his desk. He seemed neither surprised nor particularly unsettled, just a little short of breath from the exertion of the climb. He was in his fifties, Chater guessed, and was dressed in light-colored chinos, a dark shirt, and a sports jacket. His face was in shadows, but Chater could see enough to recognize that it was Strang. His expression was bland. The only thing menacing about him at all was his uncanny lack of fear.

"Ah, good," said Strang mildly. "You've brought my little darling back." He checked his watch. "And just in time," he added. "My plane leaves in less than an hour."

Chater edged away from the desk. He could kill this wimp – no sweat – but he just wanted out, the faster the better. His eyes darted over Strang's body, looking for a weapon. Nothing.

Chater made his way toward the ladder. Strang stepped back obligingly, as far as the steep slope of the roofline would allow him. He seemed almost to bow as Chater passed. Chater didn't let go of his grip on the tape dispenser. It could still be a trick.

"I found the computer," he said. "I was out near the scene—"

With an audible intake of air, Strang winced and closed his eyes. "Oh, please," he said, holding up his hand. "Save me any explanations."

Chater clammed up. In a rush, he gained the stairs. His feet barely touched a tread on his way down. In another moment, he had discarded the tape dispenser and was racing down the wide front stairway, half expecting it to open up before him and reveal some hell pit. It did not. In another instant, he was out the door. He made a conscious act of slowing his retreat once he was outside, where Gemma could see him. He even made the pretense of turning to wave at the door as he climbed into the Fiero.

"He's up there," said Gemma. She was straining to look up toward the tall, arching window of the attic. Strang was waving. The desk lamp underlit his otherwise mild face, giving his features a devilish glow. Then Gemma swung the car around and they were out of there.

Lister Strang sat and stared at the screen of the iBook. He had opened up the file and was scrolling quickly through it, correcting the odd typo, noting infelicities he would work out on the plane. But all in all, it was a good little tale. He reached the end and smiled. The work was signed by Michael M. Chater. This would never do. He highlighted the name and pressed the Delete button.

Gemma chatted away happily. Chater was quiet, but that was cool. He was a writer, after all – moody, perhaps, but a kindred spirit. When the time was ripe, she would show him some of her own stuff. Why not? She turned to the passenger seat and gasped, almost lost control of the car. Before her eyes, he vanished.

The Man on the Tip

Paul Finch

I cannot think about Grandad without remembering the incident on Moss Row Tip. Not that it was a real tip, or garbage dump, as such – more a bleak stretch of derelict land littered with ash and the rusty iron bones of old industries. There were a lot of places like that around Manchester back in 1965, but Moss Row was the most impressive. It ran for about two miles in all directions, and was covered with ridges and craters and the gutted ruins of buildings.

Perhaps that's why the film crew chose it.

Our house fronted onto the tip, so we were among the first to hear them. It was a Saturday, mid-morning, and I was in the front room watching our small black-and-white when I heard the wagons outside. The next thing I knew, the whole street had turned out on the pavement to watch bobbies rope off the tip and advise everyone to keep back.

Maybe ten trucks in all had pulled up and were now dis-gorging all sorts of people and equipment. Everywhere you looked, there were men taking measurements or setting up lights on poles. Cameras appeared on tripods; a couple of

trailers with prefab cabins on the back were drawn up; and far
out on the tip, on a low ridge, people were unraveling coils
of rusty barbed wire and hammering wooden sticks in.

Only when the soldiers arrived did we get some inkling
of what it all was about. Even at my young age, I knew these
weren't modern soldiers. They were dressed in khaki and
heavy boots, but they carried old-fashioned rifles with bay-
onets and wore tin helmets. Some even had sheepskin coats
under their fretting straps. And it was obvious they weren't
real. For one thing, they didn't stand at attention, but
instead waited around in groups, laughing and talking and
smoking cigarettes. I heard a neighbor saying something
about it being nearly fifty years since the Battle of the
Somme, and explaining that this was a reconstruction for a
television documentary.

They really went to town on the details. By lunchtime, gray
smoke was drifting across the neighborhood from thunder
flashes that they'd scattered all over the ridge, and the sound
effects were equally impressive: an ongoing rattle of machine
guns and thump of artillery. A few mothers were a little concerned about that and grabbed all their kids together, but one
of the TV men – a bloke with headphones on – laughed and
told us not to worry. There was no live ammunition being
used, he said. Everything was imitation.

The men dressed as soldiers soon got involved. There
must have been fifty of them at least, and they made
repeated charges toward the ridge. Every time they got
there, all the sound effects would start in full, the smoke
would billow out, and the actors would start dying before
our very eyes, throwing their arms up and screaming, going
down in heaps.

Always, though, an older man in a raincoat and boots
would walk across, shouting: "Cut, cut, cut!" Then all around

him, the troops would get up again and walk back to the cabins, where a little stall had been set up to provide them with tea in paper cups.

It was early afternoon, and they must've been making their ninth or tenth charge of the day, when I saw Grandad coming down the street. He'd been out since the crack of dawn and had missed it all. He was very stiff and had to walk with a stick, my grandad, but on this occasion he wasn't even watching where he was going – he was too busy staring at the tip, his eyes almost popping from his head. The actors had just got up to the ridge again, and were trying to climb through the wire. The flashes and bangs started and they flopped down, one after another, shrieking in agony.

Grandad could hardly believe what he was seeing. He stopped about two houses from our own to watch, and even though I ran up to him and took his hand, he couldn't speak. When it was all over, he'd gone white as a ghost. Finally, he looked down. "What's all this, lass?"

"It's the Battle of the Somme, Grandad," I told him eagerly. "Isn't that where you were? Mum said it was."

He didn't answer, but looked cross and glared back at the events on the tip before going straight into our house and slamming the front door behind him.

Later on, when I went back in, I heard him upstairs, banging about in his room. He usually banged about in there when he was angry – that was normally after he'd lost on the dogs, though. Mum was in the kitchen making tea, so I went through and asked her what was wrong.

She didn't say anything for a minute, and outside I could still hear the phony gunfire, even though it was starting to get dark – it was like Bonfire Night.

"Your grandad didn't have a very nice time during that war, love," she finally said. "In fact, it was horrible. A lot of his friends got killed. One in particular. He doesn't like being reminded about it."

I hated seeing Grandad upset, and decided there and then that I wouldn't mention it again. I just wished the TV people would pack up and go home, but somebody outside had said they'd be there for another two or three days yet. I climbed the stairs and went along the landing to the front bedroom. My dad had been gone a long time by then, so I shared that room with Mum. I was surprised to find Grandad in there, though, now in his woolly cardigan and slippers, standing by the window, staring out at the battle.

I felt there was nothing else I could do but go and join him. It was getting misty outside, as well as dark. The actors were so caked in mud that you couldn't tell one from another, and three or four imitation wrecked vehicles had been set on fire, so there was a strong smell of oil and burning in the air. I looked up at Grandad. He had a glazed expression on his face, and every time one of those actors threw up his hands and screamed, I saw him wince.

Suddenly, he turned and looked down at me. He was a tall man, and even though white-haired and stooped, he could look very solemn and stern if he wanted to. That usually came only in church on Sundays, but I got it on this occasion as well. "It was much, much worse than this, you know," he said.

I nodded but didn't reply.

"By the end of that first day, you couldn't walk for dead men," he went on. "And they were all people you knew, lass. It wasn't like strangers whom you didn't care about." His bottom lip started to tremble. "One of them was a very good friend of mine. Barney. The best pal I ever had, I reckon . . ."

I couldn't believe that I was about to see Grandad cry — *my* grandad, who'd first been a soldier, then had worked for forty years on the coal face at Agecroft Colliery. Thankfully, I didn't see him cry, because Mum suddenly burst in carrying a bundle of laundry and immediately started to tell him off. He went grumpily downstairs, and Mum followed, ordering me to wash my hands and face and come down for tea in five minutes.

I remember standing by the window a little longer, watching the television people. They seemed to have finished for the day and were starting to clear up. The actors were all talking together and laughing, smoking more cigarettes. I noticed that when they took off their helmets, a lot of them had longish, wavy hair, like Mick Jagger or Ringo Starr. Grandad would've approved even less if he'd seen that.

He was downstairs, meanwhile, having words with Mum.

"You know there was nothing I could do, Maureen," he was saying. "There was nothing nobody could've done."

"I know, Dad," Mum said back to him in that patient-but-tired voice of hers. "I wish you'd stop talking about it, though. It's all over and done with now."

"I don't talk about it that much!" he said gruffly.

"Every now and then," she said. "But once is enough. It's over now. There's nothing you can do about it."

"Maybe I could've done," he said. "If I'd had the guts."

"Oh, for God's sake, Dad! What do you mean by 'guts'? You were only eighteen! It was hardly a matter of guts."

Grandad didn't say anything for a while, but when he did it was very soft. "I could hear him crying out, you know, pet. Calling my name, over and over again. All that night it went on. And I just lay there in the trench, listening to it. And did nothing about it."

I was nervous about going down for tea that evening, but when I did I was surprised to find everything all right. Grandad was even friendlier than usual, and he gave me a cuddle when we sat at the kitchen table. Later, when Mum and I settled down in front of the TV, Grandad joined us.

Mum looked at him suspiciously and asked why he wasn't going out to the Legion like he usually did. He made an excuse about not feeling up to it, but then spent two hours shifting restlessly in his armchair. Only much later did he go for his coat and cap and say that he'd go and have a couple of quick stouts after all.

Mum and I had both been in bed a good while when we heard him coming back. His stick clicking along the pavement was a very familiar sound to me on Saturday nights, and I always knew that it was okay to go to sleep when I heard that. This time he didn't come straight inside, though, and after a minute, puzzled, I went to the window and moved the curtain to have a look out.

Grandad was on the other side of the road, gazing out over the tip. The moon was up, and it all gleamed wetly in a ghostly radiance – every piece of rubble burnished with silver, every coil of wire, every ridge and pit and pool of water. Grandad was standing there on the edge of it, like a statue of black iron.

For some reason, I decided that he wouldn't be angry if I went out there with him, so I put on my duffle coat over my pajamas and a pair of boots, and I crept downstairs. The front door was only on the latch, so I let myself out and walked across the road. Grandad looked round but didn't seem surprised to see me. We both stood there for a moment, watching. The smell of acrid smoke had still not gone away – in fact, it seemed stronger and made me want to cough.

"Did you hear it, lass?" he finally asked me in a whisper.

"Hear what, Grandad?"

"Listen . . . you'll hear it," he said.

We listened for a moment or two, and I heard nothing.

"There!" Grandad suddenly hissed. "Did you hear it that time?"

I didn't know what to say, but now Grandad seemed excited. I strained my ears but still heard nothing.

And then, suddenly . . .

"Arthur . . . Arthur, please . . ."

I heard it! Very weak and seemingly far away, but I distinctly heard it. I looked up at Grandad, bewildered. But he seemed transported with joy and seized me by the shoulder. "Come on, pet," he said. "I'll need you. But keep low."

And he set off onto the tip, moving with more agility than I'd ever realized he was capable of. I had to trot to keep up, but I was soon plowing through thick, treacly mud and heaps of broken bricks. Grandad took it all in his stride, however, constantly encouraging me with words like "That's a good lass, keep up," or "You're doing great, but if I say 'duck,' duck."

We got to the ridge almost immediately, and all over it I could see holes in the ground where the thunder flashes had been buried. Smoke was still wisping out of some of them. Grandad wasn't content yet, though. He started to batter the barbed wire with his walking stick in big, sweeping, angry strokes. "Always was a bugger, this stuff," he grunted, sweat gleaming on his brow.

"Grandad," I said, "you're going to hurt yourself."

If he heard me, he gave no sign. I remember looking back and seeing our house on the other side of the streetlights, just one in an unbroken wall of red-brick two-up, two-downs.

Then that voice came to us again, from somewhere just ahead. "Arthur . . ." it wailed pathetically.

"I'm coming, lad," Grandad said, and taking my hand, he pressed on, stepping over the flattened wire, telling me to be careful with it.

We started down a steep hill, over more slippery rubble. At the bottom of it, a large puddle glittered in the moonlight.

"Got your boots on, I hope!" Grandad said. He was breathing very hard.

I nodded but hardly had a chance to speak, for he suddenly went down on one knee, clutching at his chest, making a rasping, wheezing sound. His eyes looked as if they were about to pop out of his head. I felt his hand go cold in mine.

I was frozen for a second, not knowing what to do, when right behind us a thunder flash went off! I remember looking round to the top of the ridge as a plume of fire spurted up into the air, twenty feet or more. I felt the loose ground shaking beneath me.

The next thing I knew, though, Grandad was back on his feet and urging me to hurry. I asked him if he was okay, and he said he was. We waded through the puddle and found ourselves in a morass of mud, which slowed us down even more. It was almost over the tops of my boots! Not too far away, I thought I heard what sounded like a car backfiring. Somehow, though, I knew it wasn't that. If it was, it backfired several times more over the next few minutes – and from the other side of the tip, two or three other cars started backfiring in direct response.

The ground rose steeply in front of us again, and we almost had to crawl. By the time we got to the top of that one, I was absolutely whacked. I didn't know how Grandad could cope. Just before we plunged down into the next valley, I looked around and saw another thunder flash go off about half a mile away. It lit up the landscape in a blood red glare, and again the ground shook. There was now a terrible smell about the place, and then I heard a machine gun start up.

"Arthur . . ." the voice pleaded again. It seemed closer now but a lot weaker.

"Not so far," Grandad said. We followed a narrow gully through another fence of barbed wire.

I'd never realized the tip was so big, because we then came out over more open ground and all I could see for miles was the ravaged terrain and jet black sky. Occasionally, a light would streak across it, and somewhere in the distance we'd hear a shrill scream followed by a loud thump.

"Arthur?" said the voice, quite close to us.

"I'm here, lad, stop your fretting," Grandad replied.

Over the next rise, we found a figure curled up in a crater. At first, I thought it was a dummy. He was so plastered in mud from head to toe that I couldn't identify him as a living man. He was, though, because as we scrambled down to him, he started to move.

He didn't say much as we helped him up, just whimpered, but he managed to get one arm around each of our necks and limped badly as we walked him back. If the outward trip had been bad, the return was infinitely worse. Grandad was constantly telling us to get down as machine guns suddenly started to hammer and objects whistled over our heads. The mud, swimming around our knees, seemed more like porridge, and the smells were now an unbearable stench that lingered everywhere. We pressed bravely on despite all, and gradually it began to fall behind us.

At last, we came to that first ridge and the lines of wire put up by the television people. The ground seemed firmer underfoot there, the air sweeter. I could still hear the thump and crash of guns, but they were far in the background. By the time we got to the edge of the road, I could hardly hear anything.

I was utterly worn out, too physically drained even to worry what Mum was going to say about the state of my pajamas. The man from the tip was now a dead weight on my arm. It was a good thing that Grandad was doing most of the carrying.

When we got to the front step, he stood back and, while I opened the door, actually lifted the man up over his shoulder like a fireman would. Then he carried him inside by himself, moving straight into the darkened front room and placing him on the couch. I was amazed how strong he was.

"You're a good lass," he said to me as he leaned over the man and loosened his tunic. "Now get on upstairs to bed, eh? Best not let your mum catch you up at this hour."

I knew he was right. I took one look back into the room before I went. Grandad stood up again, and I saw him silhouetted against the window. I'd never realized what a firm jaw he had, what a sturdy neck and big shoulders.

"Go on, pet," he said in a gentle voice. I did.

When I awoke the next day, I rushed to my window and looked out over Moss Row Tip. I expected to see them filming more battle scenes in the early morning light. But instead of the flash of artillery and crackle of gunfire, the tip was alive with flashing lights and radio static. An ambulance and police cars were parked all over as the film crew stood idly by.

I found out later that morning what had happened, but I never believed that the man they found lying out on the tip, one hand on his heart, was Grandad. You see, I still see him. Even now. Him and his mate. In the pub, down at the bookie's. They're inseparable. Always so cheerful, always winking. It gives me a nice, warm feeling inside when I see them. It's just a shame I'm the only one who does.

To Be More Like Them

Edo van Belkom

She got onto the school bus, took her usual spot directly behind the driver, then sunk down in the seat until she knew she couldn't be seen by the kids at the back.

Those were the popular kids.

The cool kids.

And although they were as far away from her as the bus would allow, they were never far from her thoughts. In fact, they were always on her mind, gnawing at it like rats on cheese.

Her name was Sherry Lace. A decidedly beautiful name, one that she'd been proud of as a little girl.

"What's your name, honey?"

"Sherry Lace."

"My, but isn't that pretty?"

"Uh-huh."

"Aren't you gonna knock 'em dead when you get older?"

"Uh-huh."

A pretty name, except that it just happened to rhyme with Scary Face, which is what all the kids called her now. Although the nickname rhymed with her own, they weren't being clever. It didn't take much thought or imagination to turn Sherry Lace into Scary Face when she had a scar that started just under her right eye, went across the tip of her nose, and curved around her cheek all the way to her left ear. In addition to the skin, several muscles had been cut and nerve endings damaged, and although the scar had already had six months to heal, it still looked red and fresh. It was sore too, making it painful for her to talk and agony for her to laugh. It hurt even to smile.

It also made it hard for her to go out in public. She would have dropped out of school if they'd let her, but all the adults had convinced her to tough it out, saying it wouldn't be that bad.

But it *was* that bad. Worse than bad. Every day was a nightmare.

"It's getting better every day, hon."

"A little bit of makeup and you can hardly tell."

"The kids will understand."

Yeah, right.

The kids understood. They understood that she was a freak, a monster, a walking wound.

Scary Face, they called her, to her face and behind her back. They understood just fine, and they wanted nothing to do with her.

She was on the outside looking in.

She had always been there too, even before the scar.

She'd never been pretty enough to be part of the cool group. She'd never been smart enough to be one of the brainers. And she'd never had the physical strength or coordination to be an athlete. She'd dressed in black, thinking she might be able to join the goths, but they didn't want her either, which hurt most of all, since most of them were rejects from the other cliques themselves.

Even the geeks teased her, as if they knew that by teasing her, they would deflect some of the ridicule from themselves, be part of a group, the group that teased Scary Face. Anyone could join, no membership required. All you had to be able to do was laugh at your classmate and sleep soundly through the night.

Everyone was part of that group – everyone but her.

The bus came to a stop and four more kids got on. The bus was filling up now, and space was getting tight. One of the boys getting on – Bill, she thought his name was – searched the length of the bus for an empty seat.

She moved over to make room for him, but he just kept standing there, looking for an empty seat with the others farther down the bus.

"Sit down," said the bus driver.

"But I—"

"Sit down!" the driver repeated, this time with even more authority.

With a sigh, Bill sat down next to her, not looking too pleased about having to sit next to Scary Face.

Maybe he thinks he'll catch something, she mused, like a scar. Or maybe he'll be contaminated by the loser bug and suddenly find himself with her, on the outside looking in.

"Billy," whispered a voice behind her.

She wanted to turn around to see who was talking, but she knew that if she did, one of the kids at the back would greet her with an angry look and the words "What are you looking at, ugly?" It was so much easier to do nothing.

When the bus came to a stop at the next light, Bill was gone, hurrying down the aisle before the bus started moving or the driver noticed he was out of his seat.

And so she was alone again. It was actually better this way. After the brief moment of hope was gone – the one in which she thought that maybe, just maybe, he was sitting next to her because he wanted to, or because, hey, it was no big deal – it had become painful to have him sitting next to her, knowing that he'd rather be somewhere else, anywhere else, even under the wheels, instead of sitting up at the front behind the driver and next to Scary Face.

"God, how could you stand it, being next to *her*," they would say when he finally reached the others. "How could you stand it?"

It made her laugh as much as it made her cry.

If they couldn't handle being in the seat next to her, then what would they do if they found themselves not in the seat *next* to her but in *her* seat, in her shoes. . . .

In her face.

The school day began much like every other – alone and in silence. She made a trip to her locker, put her lunch away, and grabbed the books she'd need for the morning's classes.

Her locker was close to the door, so it was easy for her to slip into the school unnoticed, but her homeroom was at the other end of the building and getting there was like running a gauntlet each morning. Most of the kids would just whisper "Scary Face," bark like dogs, or make noises like they were about to throw up. They did it so often that she hardly heard them anymore. Sometimes, however, they could be crueler.

She was halfway to homeroom when it happened.

"Hey, Scary Face," someone called out. "What happened? Cut yourself shaving?"

Roars of laughter.

Her face turned red. Her scar began to throb.

The first impulse was always to run away, but she refused to do it. She'd never run from anything in her life, and she wasn't about to start now. She wanted to scream out, confront whoever it was who'd said that, but she'd done that only once before.

"Who said that?"

Whispers and giggles.

"Who was it?"

Silence.

"Like I thought. Too chicken-hearted to say it to my face."

"Better to have a chicken heart than a hamburger face."

More laughter.

"Scary Face. Scary Face. Scary Face."

Her lesson learned, she remained still and silent, taking it all in.

There were whispers up and down the hallway, and the words "Scary Face" seemed to linger in the air like smoke.

How could they be so cruel? How could they be so relentless in their abuse? She'd often asked herself these questions while she lay awake at night, staring at the ceiling.

The hallway slowly came back to life, with giggles and laughter bubbling up from the bottom of the whispers until someone, maybe the one with the big mouth, began howling with laughter.

The scar throbbed in pain, felt as if it had opened up and was dripping blood down her cheek. She moved forward through the crowd, heading for her homeroom, but was happy just to make it to the bathroom and a stall before she broke down and cried.

Imagine, she mused. I'd wanted to be more like *them*.

And that's when something happened inside.

The ache in her heart turned itself off, like a light switch that illuminates a room one minute then leaves it in total darkness the next.

Suddenly, there was no more pain. No more tears.

She felt as if a weight had been lifted from her shoulders. The heat was gone and the scar no longer throbbed. She went back out into the hall, and for a moment, she imagined herself walking not through a hallway full of students but through a forest of dead trees and barren soil.

It brought a smile to her face.

Even though it pained her, she smiled broadly at them all, baring her teeth in a sort of sneer.

And the noise in the hallway slowly died down until it was deathly silent, as if everyone knew that . . .

Something had gone drastically wrong with the routine.

She hadn't always had the scar.

And while she'd never really been pretty, she had looked good enough to hope that puberty might somehow transform her into a beautiful woman.

After all, her mother had been a beauty.

But her looks had been lost too, the same night she'd got the scar.

That night, her father had come home drunk. He'd done something stupid like lose his job, gamble away his paycheck, or total the car. Who knew what the problem was – it didn't matter anyway. The important thing was that he'd come home drunk, and that things would go one of two ways. He would either head upstairs, fall onto the bed, and sleep it off, or he would come into the living room looking for a fight.

Turned out to be the latter.

He'd stumbled to the doorway, leaned shakily against the frame, and said, "What the hell are you looking at?"

"Nothing."

Whether her mother had meant it sarcastically or not, Sherry was never certain. Her father had sure taken it to be a jab, however, and in minutes her parents were screaming at each other at the top of their voices, using words and calling each other names that Sherry had been told never to say herself.

While the two went at it, she had tried to sink into the couch, hoping that this fight wouldn't last too long. But the row wasn't showing any signs of ending. Instead, it was getting worse. They'd moved into the kitchen, and things were getting broken. They were pushing each other, and if it didn't stop soon, someone was going to get hurt . . . worse than usual.

And then her mother had screamed, "Put that down!"

There was fear in her voice.

Real terror.

Sherry had jumped off the couch and run into the kitchen in time to see her father standing there with a six-inch knife in his hand. He was slashing it wildly back and forth in front of her mother, getting closer to her throat with each swing.

"No, Dad. Stop!" she'd cried.

And then her father had turned to look at her. The knife had flashed across her field of vision. There was intense heat across her face, and then wet warmth running down her cheeks.

And the fight was over.

Her mother had ridden with her in the ambulance.

She'd never seen her father again.

She'd heard that he'd been roughed up pretty bad in prison. Apparently, inmates didn't relate all that well to guys who cut up their own kids.

So maybe some good had come of it.

The doctors who had sewn up her face had said that in another year, they'd be able to do some work on the scar to make it less noticeable. They'd also sent her to visit a woman who specialized in makeup for people with skin conditions and facial deformities.

Sherry had gone to see her once, but the makeup had felt heavy on her skin, had cracked when she smiled, and had left the scar red and raw the next day.

She'd cried for a long time after that.

Even the lady who fixed up freaks couldn't help her.

That night Sherry slept like a baby, the smile still lingering on her face.

In the morning, she got onto the bus refreshed and looking forward to the day. She took her usual spot directly behind the driver, but now she sat so that her head and shoulders rose up over the seat and would be in full view of the kids at the back of the bus.

If they teased her today, that would be fine with her. It might as well be today, in fact, seeing as it would be one of their last chances to do it.

After today, things were going to be different.

"Hey, Scary Face!" someone called from the back of the bus.

Sherry ignored the comment, wondering why no one could think of something better. Maybe she could come up with something, mention it to a few kids, and see if it spread through the school. Something catchy like Slice Girl or Scar-let.

Very cool.

"Scary Face," somebody whispered behind her.

Sherry turned around and smiled.

The kid behind her looked surprised at the move, his eyes growing wide with just a hint of fear.

Good, thought Sherry. Get used to it, kid. There'll be plenty more where that came from.

The kid looked away, unable to stare into Sherry's eyes for more than a few seconds. Sherry's smile widened, and she turned back around in her seat. As the bus pulled away from the stop, she slipped her hands into her knapsack and ran her fingers along the handle, then traced a finger down to the plastic cover sheathing the blade.

The police had taken the knife as evidence, then had given it back to her and her mother a few months later when the trial was over and they didn't need it anymore. At the time, Sherry had wondered why the police thought they'd want the knife back, but now she was glad they'd returned it.

She had tried to be more like them, like the kids on the bus and the kids in her school, but none of them could look past the scar and see the girl behind it. They wouldn't let her into their world because of the way she looked.

She closed the fingers of her right hand around the knife's rough wooden handle and slid the plastic cover off the blade with her left.

The bus pulled into the school and stopped.

The doors opened up to the schoolyard.

She had wanted to be more like them, but that had been wrong. She knew that now.

She tightened her grip on the knife and got off the bus.

She could never be like them, but maybe she could make *them* a little more like *her*.

About the Contributors

Nancy Etchemendy's story "Bigger Than Death" (published in *Cricket* magazine) won the 1998 Bram Stoker Award for superior achievement in a work for young readers. Her third science-fiction novel for children, *The Power of Un*, will be published in 2000. Her books and stories for both adults and young readers have been appearing regularly since 1980.

Paul Finch lives in Lancashire, England. A former police officer, he is now a full-time writer working in the horror and thriller genres. He has published some 200 short stories in anthologies and magazines in both Britain and North America. He also writes for animated television shows and for the British cop show "The Bill."

Ed Gorman has been called "one of suspense fiction's best storytellers" by *Ellery Queen* magazine and "one of the most original voices in today's crime fiction" by the *San Diego Union*. A resident of Cedar Rapids, Iowa, Gorman has published stories in every magazine from *Redbook* to *Poetry Today*.

He has won numerous awards, including the Spur Award (for his westerns), the Shamus (for his private-eye novels), and the International Fiction Writer's Award.

Ed Greenwood is a fantasy and science-fiction writer who lives in a book-filled farmhouse near Cobourg, Ontario. He's the creator of the Forgotten Realms, perhaps the most detailed fantasy world yet. Greenwood has written just over 100 books and just under 500 magazine articles, columns, and short stories, which have sold millions of copies worldwide in more than twenty languages and won him numerous awards. But, he says, he'd trade it all for magic that really works.

Monica Hughes is the author of more than thirty novels, and has twice won the Canada Council Prize (now the Governor General's Literary Award for Children's Text). She lives in Edmonton, Alberta, now but has spent time in England, Scotland, Zimbabwe, and Egypt. Although she's best known for writing science fiction (and edited an anthology of science-fiction and fantasy writing called *What If . . . ?*), she was eager to explore the darker side of fiction with "The Gift," her first tale of horror.

Michael Kelly is the author of more than twenty short stories, including one that appeared in *Canadian Fiction* magazine's all-horror issue and two others that garnered honorable mentions in *The Year's Best Fantasy and Horror*, an annual anthology. He lives with his wife, the poet Carolyn Macdonell, and their two children in Pickering, Ontario.

Montreal's **Nancy Kilpatrick** is originally from Philadelphia. Winner of the Arthur Ellis Award, Kilpatrick is best known as a writer of vampire tales and as the author of the novels *Near Death*, *Reborn*, *Child of the Night*, *As One Dead* (with Don Bassingthwaite), and *Dracul*. She is also an accomplished editor, and has two anthologies to her credit, *In the Shadow of the Gargoyle* and *Graven Images* (co-edited with Thomas Roche).

Joe R. Lansdale has won many awards for his horror fiction, including the Bram Stoker Award, presented by the Horror Writers Association. A resident of Texas, he has written hundreds of mystery, suspense, fantasy, and western stories; dozens of novels, including a Batman novel for young adults; and story collections such as *By Bizarre Hands*, *Bestsellers Guaranteed*, and *Writers of the Purple Rage*.

Richard Laymon is the author of more than thirty novels of horror and suspense that have been published in fifteen languages around the world. His first and best-known book, *The Cellar*, was published in 1980 and has often been cited as one of the best horror novels of all time. His more recent titles include *Bite*, *Quake*, and *Savage*. Some of the Los Angeles resident's more than sixty-five short stories can be found in the collection *Fiends*.

Scott Nicholson works as a newspaper reporter in the mountains of North Carolina. He has sold stories to *Aboriginal SF*, *Carpe Noctern*, *Dead Promises*, *More Monsters from Memphis*, and other publications. He placed first overall in the Writers of the Future Contest in 1998. A story collection, *Thank You for the Flowers*, is on the way in 2000. Nicholson maintains a writer's area on his Web site at users.boone.net/nicholson.

Since 1988, **Edmund Plante** has published twenty-three young adult horror novels with the German publisher Cora Verlag. In North America, he's published two horror novels for young readers, *Alone in the House* and *Last Date*, and several adult novels, such as *Garden of Evil* and *Trapped*. A resident of Webster, Massachusetts, he has also had many short stories published in such magazines as the *Portland Review*, *Haunts*, and *Dark Regions*.

Steve Rasnic Tem has published stories in such young adult anthologies as *A Nightmare's Dozen* and *Bruce Coville's Spine Tinglers II*. His work has also appeared in the *Magazine of Fantasy and Science Fiction*, *Isaac Asimov's SF Magazine*, *365 Scary Stories*, *The Year's Best Fantasy and Horror*, and many other publications. A collection of the Colorado resident's short stories, *City Fishing*, recently appeared from Silver Salamander Press.

Thornhill, Ontario's **Robert J. Sawyer** is the only writer to win the top science-fiction awards of the United States (the Nebula), France (the Grand Prix de l'Imaginaire), Spain (Premio UPC de Ciencia Ficción), and Japan (Seiun). In addition, he was won the Aurora for both his short fiction and his novels, as well as the Arthur Ellis Award from the Crime Writers of Canada for best short story. His eleven novels include *The Terminal Experiment*, *Factoring Humanity*, and *Flashforward*. For more information about him and his work, visit his Web site at www.sfwriter.com.

Edo van Belkom has won both the Bram Stoker Award and the Aurora Award for his short stories. His more than 150 short stories have been published in everything from *Truck News* to *Year's Best Horror Stories* 20. His many books include the novels *Wyrm Wolf*, *Lord Soth*, *Mister Magick*, and *Teeth*; the short-story collection *Death Drives a Semi*; and a book of interviews, *Northern Dreamers*. He lives in Brampton, Ontario, and his Web page is located at www.vanbelkom.com.

Tim Wynne-Jones has written radio plays, opera librettos, lyrics for musicals, songs, picture books, and novels. He has won the Governor General's Literary Award for Children's Text twice: in 1993 for *Some of the Kinder Planets* and again in 1995 for *The Maestro*. About his story "The iBook," he says, "About two weeks after I began writing this story, my house was broken into while I was out West at a book festival. Unlike [what happens in] my story, the thieves did not make it up to my loft, and therefore did not steal my computer (an elderly Mac LC III). Had they done so, they probably would not have actually read any of the stories there, least of all this one. Too bad."